GENTLY CALL
and
SOFTLY RISE

Stories
by

Dave McCauley

This is a work of fiction. The characters, incidents and dialogues are products of the author's imagination and are not to be construed as real. Any resemblance to actual events or persons, living or dead, is entirely coincidental.

Also by Dave McCauley

A FAIR IN TIME - Adventures in the Turkey Capital of the World

DEDICATION

To the memory of my wife, Ilona, a helper, advisor and loving companion on our life's journey; too soon snatched away. My daughter, Susan Schirmers, who has worked hard to help me through the dark days and selflessly put up with my many whims and failures and goaded me into action when I needed goading.

CONTENTS

FORWARD

Because I write mostly for my own enjoyment, I am free to undertake whatever whim comes my way. I have divided those whims into two groups, so the reader won't be mystified by a jumble.

The first group; Short Stories, are made-up fiction with the exception of "One Sunday Morning" which is loosely based on the loss of my cousin in Laos during the Vietnam War. The following "Primrose Tales" are loosely based on stories of from my mother's childhood. Growing up in Nebraska at the beginning of the nineteen hundreds.

A Coffee House Dream

It was only a short walk to my car from the warm office where I'd left a group of smiling and unctuous men who sought to engage me for their profit. I had hoped their proposal would give me a chance to enjoy a comfortable new year, but alas, they proposed a scheme involving deceit and chicanery. I was disappointed and angry that they sought to take advantage of me. My holiday had not been as festive as I'd hoped and with the chance of starting the year off with a much-needed contract slipping away my cheerful expectations dimmed. In the end, we shook hands, wished each other a Happy New Year and parted, they back into the cozy, sweet larceny of their lair and I into the sunlit crystal cold of the last afternoon in December. I felt relieved to be on my way, free of their blandishments; None the less I had lost the festive holiday mood and walked slowly, dejectedly, head down, hands jammed into my coat pockets wondering where life would lead me next.

As I neared my car, a delightful aroma turned my head and drew me off the street and into the warmth of a crowded and noisy coffee house. I ordered a large latte' and looked for an empty chair where I could contemplate my future.

I found a vacant seat across from a newspaper over which a rising column of smoke suggested a reader concealed behind the barrier of newsprint. As I sat down, the paper slowly lowered, revealing the smoker, a slight, middle-aged man with thinning brown hair and soft grey eyes, a cigarette dangling carelessly from the corner of his mouth. He surveyed me intently for a moment and then took the cigarette out of his mouth and stubbed it out.

"Do you believe in dreams?" He asked softly, his gaze fixed on my face. "I mean in dreams that actually happened."

For some reason I wasn't surprised by such a question from a complete stranger. Maybe I was buoyed by my exhilarating walk and gave some slight nod of encouragement. Anyway, he continued as though I'd begged him for more.

"I live alone. No family around here anymore." He lit another cigarette and paused putting the paper down. "I work in the warehouse across the street."

He leaned forward to emphasize the seriousness of his intimate revelations. I took a drink of my Latte'. I've heard some great stories of unique and exotic experiences from panhandlers, but he didn't look like he was about to hit me up for money; didn't look like his dreams came in pills or out of bottles either; so, I pulled my chair a little closer.

"A warehouse," I said signaling my willingness for him to continue.

"On Christmas Eve they gave us all turkeys and then we got off two hours early, with pay. I don't have no way to fix a turkey so I gave it to one of the other guys who said he could use it. His brother has lots of kids, I guess. Anyway, on the way home -- I live over by Loring Park and take the bus -- I got a take-out pizza and six pack of beer." He stopped talking and looked at his cigarette as though he was replaying that afternoon in the column of rising smoke.

I wondered what his place looked like, a couple of threadbare, dimly lit rooms maybe. He didn't look poor though; so maybe I've heard "A CHRISTMAS CAROLE" too many times.

"Not much to do on Christmas Eve. I ate my pizza, drank a couple of beers and watched TV for a while. Fell asleep I guess, watching TV." He paused again, closing his eyes.

"It was snowing," he continued his voice lowered. "Big fluffy flakes, floating straight down, no sound at all. I couldn't see anything except those snowflakes. I couldn't really tell where I was, but that didn't matter. I just walked along in the snow. I was warm and felt good, happy too. I walked and walked, it was beautiful with the lights and all. A ways ahead of me I saw a little girl standing under a streetlight. When I got closer, I could see she didn't have on a hat or coat, just a robe or something like that. I thought she was lost so I walked up to her and asked if she needed help. She said no, she was waiting for Christmas to come. That seemed okay to me, so I said I was too. I started to walk away, and she just took my hand and walked along with me. Somehow, we ended up over at the Basilica. There were lots of people going in. Midnight Mass: I did that once. I looked at her and she nodded so we walked up the steps and went right in. The place was packed, and people were standing on the sides, but we just walked right up front and sat down. Everyone was singing and a whole bunch of guys came down the center ringing bells and carrying a big tent like thing and the choir followed them down singing <u>Silent Night</u>. The girl and I just sang along and prayed with everyone else. It was grand. When it was over, and we were getting ready to leave the girl tugged my sleeve and said we should give each other a present because it was Christmas. I felt around in my pockets; I didn't have anything except a little silver whistle that I found a couple of days before; you know like a referee's whistle. I held it out and she took it. Then she took off a Christmas wreath pin she had on her robe and handed it to me and said Merry Christmas."

He stopped talking to light another cigarette. I wondered what the next chapter would bring.

"It was still dark when I woke up in my chair in front of the TV; almost three o'clock in the morning. I just went to bed and that's the dream."

We sat quietly, each contemplating the other. At last, he folded up the paper, stubbed out his cigarette, stood up and pulled on his coat. As he pushed back his chair, he drew another newspaper out of his coat pocket and slid it across the table toward me. He then started to search through his coat pockets, locating an object, he took it out and dropped it on top of the folded-up newspaper. With that he turned, pushed open the coffee house door and was gone.

Lying on the newspaper was a little green plastic Christmas wreath with a clasp pin on the back. I fingered it for a moment and then looked down at the paper.

MANY ESCAPE APARTMENT FIRE
GIRL'S BRAVE ACTION
GETS CREDIT

A Christmas Eve fire sent two dozen families out into the snow last night at the Oak Grove Apartments near Loring Park. Fire Captain Bob Camp, said quick thinking by a young girl prevented injuries and probably saved lives. The girl alerted everyone in the burning building by running up and down the halls blowing a whistle and knocking on doors.

Nine year old Susan Harris offered a strange explanation for her heroic effort. "I was dreaming that an angel took me to Midnight Mass and when I woke up I was outside and there was fire in the basement." When asked where she got the whistle, Susan answered, "from the angel I guess."

The Little Girl who could Fly

Doug's parents bought their first house in 1962, a modest two-bedroom home on Prairie Street close to the edge of town. It wasn't a very remarkable place, but it sure beat the apartment they left behind. The house was most likely built in the 1920's and must have predated running water and plumbing in that neighborhood because the bathroom was in the basement and there was a well in the back yard with a long-handled pump. The most unique feature of their new home was its bedroom closets, both of which were connected; go into one bedroom closet, push your way past the clothes hangers, turn left and you were the other bedroom closet! Not much of a feature, but to an almost eight-year-old boy it was a fascinating feature.

There were lots of kids in the neighborhood and school was out for the summer so Douglas and his brother, George, made friends quickly. Because they were on the edge of town there was room to roam and plenty of vacant space to play. Most of the time the boys played a version of baseball called work-up. If the batter was out or got a hit, he moved to first base and everyone moved over one position, the catcher became the batter next, and the pitcher became the catcher. Douglas was poorly equipped to play baseball. His right eye had astigmatism and didn't focus very well so he had no depth perception which meant he couldn't catch or hit. To make matters worse, he had a rubber arm and couldn't throw very well either. Whenever the gang began gathering baseball mitts and bats Douglas started looking for an escape plan.

Right across the street from the Lang house was a large two-story house occupied by the Johnson family. Their only child was a girl named Margalene. Douglas met Margalene a few days after his family arrived in the neighborhood. He saw her sitting on their front step, crossed the street and said hello. Margalene and Douglas were about the same size. She was slender with brown hair and lively brown eyes and a dimple on her chin. Her eyebrows were dark and nearly met in the middle of her forehead which gave her a fierce looking scowl when she was angry. Douglas noticed that she talked slowly and sounded like she was chewing her words. He told her he was going into third grade in the fall and asked what grade she was in.

"I have to go to school at home. My mom teaches me."

"Why can't you go to school?" he asked. He'd never heard of home schooling before.

"Because sometimes I fly and could hurt myself."

"You can fly! How do you do that?" He was astonished.

"I can't really fly, but that's what my mother calls it. Sometimes I just faint and fall over. I wear a cap in the house, and everything is moved out of the way so I usually don't hit anything in the house, but school would be too dangerous." She smiled. "Let's go to the back yard." Margalene reached over, grabbed his hand and stood up.

The Johnson house must have been a farm home at one time; there was a storage shed behind their garage and a small pasture behind the shed. A swing hung from a large maple tree in the center of the backyard, and they had a teeter-totter too. Doug and Margalene walked hand in hand around the house and into the back yard. Margalene's mother came out the back door and met them.

"Hello. Are you one of the new boys across the street?

"Yes, my name is Douglas and I'm going to be in third grade this fall."

Margalene's mother smiled and sat down on the backstep.

"I'm glad to meet you, but I have to tell about our rules when you come over here to play."

She went on to explain that there was no running, jumping or climbing and you needed to get permission to leave their yard. She told him that Margalene sometimes fell down quickly for no reason and that he should hold her hand when they walked. Douglas shook his head yes, but didn't say anything.

"I already told Doug that we call it flying." Margalene gave Douglas a friendly shove and smiled.

Her mother laughed, got up and went inside.

Douglas later came to understand that Margalene's parents were very protective of her, but didn't want her to be stigmatized as having seizures or what most people called "fits" and were trying hard to minimize the seriousness of her condition; keeping her safe and at the same time letting her enjoy a more normal childhood. That may explain why her mother trusted him with their daughter. There weren't too many girls his age in the neighborhood which meant Margalene didn't have a lot of playmates, so she and Douglas were often together. Summer is a time of freedom and Margalene's restrictions should have greatly limited her choice of activities, but the two of them often bent the rules. In the backyard shed there was a ladder that let up to a loft and they delighted in climbing up into the dim recesses and wandering around the collection of useless castoffs. The loft was usually very hot so that exploration never lasted very long. They escaped the back yard one day by crawling under the barbed wire fence that enclosed the small pasture. Douglas soon became aware that others had been there before; he made this discovery by stepping in a "cow pie." They never escaped into the pasture again.

Douglas didn't spend all his time playing with Margalene. There weren't always enough boys around to make up the nine players needed to field a full squad for baseball games, so he was often dragooned into playing. Along with his older brother, George, they took swimming lessons at the lake three mornings a week and usually hung around the beach for a while before coming home. Living at the edge of town meant the troop of boys were able to easily slip into the open fields and wander along the jungle of weeds that bordered the drainage ditch dividing the farmland. There was a railroad track the ran northward out of town and once a day a small freight train would grumble along those tracks announcing its passing with metallic blats from it horn. If the gang was nearby when they heard the train coming, they'd scramble along the drainage ditch and crowd under the tiny railroad bridge and listen with delight as the train rumbled overhead.

Douglas hadn't been over to the Johnson's for a few days and hadn't seen Margalene outside so one morning he decided to go over to see if she wanted to come out and play. As he walked up the sidewalk Mrs. Johnson opened the front door.

"Oh Doug, you're just the boy I've been looking for. I have a few things to put on the curb for the junk man and I'd like some help carrying them. Will you help me?"

He nodded yes. She walked down the front steps and led him around the house to the garage. They pulled out a broken coaster-wagon, a garden cart with only one wheel and an old garbage can full of flowerpot pieces and other junk which they dragged to the curb. As they worked Margalene came out and sat down on the front step to watch. When they finished, Douglass sat down next to her.

"Don't leave, I'll be right back." Mrs. Johnson disappeared inside and quickly returned.

"Here's something for your help." She handed him a quarter.

The sky was deep blue, and the sun was already high so it was quickly getting hot. Squeezing the newfound wealth of the quarter, feeling the heat of the day and getting thirsty gave him a sudden urge.

"Can I take Margalene up to Brown's store for a Popsicle?"

"Oh Mom, can he?" Margalene blurted out excitedly.

"Of course he can. "Mrs. Johnson looked at him and pursed her lips. "Douglas, you have to hold Margalene's hand all the way to the store and back. Please don't let her fall. Can you do that? Can I trust you?"

He nodded earnestly.

"Yippee," squealed Margalene clapping her hands.

"Don't drip on your dress." Mrs. Johnson called as they walked away.

The two of them walked hand in hand the block to Brown's store. The Popsicles where a dime each; Margalene chose cherry flavor and Doug picked orange. They sat on the shaded bench outside the store and ate the rapidly melting treats and then walked back. Their hands were pretty sticky from the Popsicle juice which made them laugh as they walked along stuck to each other. Back to Margalene's house they both went inside and washed their hands in the Johnson's kitchen sink. Then Margalene told him that she always had to go lie down for a while after being outside so Douglas went home happy that they'd had an adventure and that nothing bad happened.

Douglas knew that Margalene's parents never wanted her away from their sight, sending her beyond their reach even for one block must have been stressful for Mrs. Johnson. Somehow, she trusted him, but he still didn't know why. As far as he knew, the cause of her collapses was unknown and that meant her recovery was always uncertain. What if she didn't just wake up? Added to the separation was the chance of injury. Many of her falls resulted in bad bruises and even a couple of broken bones; so, their trip to Brown's store was exciting for everyone involved.

Margalene "flew" only once while Douglas was with her. They were going to the house next door to Johnson's to look at a pear tree, wondering if the pears were ripening. The pear tree owners had given all the kids in the neighborhood permission to pick pears and eat them. So, they headed from Johnson's to the backyard next door, hoping the time was "ripe." As they walked in the grass toward the pear tree, Margalene stumbled a little and then just collapsed.

Doug was holding her hand, and she almost pulled him down as she fell, landing at his feet in a motionless heap. Douglas panicked and didn't know what to do; he just stood there frozen, hanging onto her hand. As he let go of her hand and started to turn to run to her house, he heard her say "Now what?" He stopped and knelt down, still panicked.

"Do you need to go home?" He grabbed her hand.

She looked up and shook her head.

"Are you okay? Can you get up?"

She sat up and shook herself.

"I think I just went flying." She looked at him with that fierce scowl.

He sat down next to her.

"What's it like?"

"I don't remember anything. I'm walking and then I'm lying on the grass. Sometimes I'm dizzy for a bit after I wake up. That's because I often hit my head hard." She rolled her eyes and smiled.

He was relieved to see her smile. She stood up, grabbed his hand and pulled him toward the pear tree. The pears weren't even close to being ripe. As they turned away to head back to her house she stopped.

"I remember flying once" she exclaimed. "Everything was blue - grass, houses, people, even flowers. I was high in the sky and could soar around like a bird. I was so happy and excited I laughed. Mom said I was laughing when I came back."

He walked her back to their house, and she went inside to lie down. She never flew again when he was with her.

Summer passes slowly when you're young; the days are uniformly tranquil. The Lang family wasn't wealthy enough to go on summer jaunts or have a speed boat or a cabin at the lake. So, the boys made do, work-up baseball games, playing in the drainage ditches, walking to the fairgrounds, going to the park by the lake and going to the library. Douglas didn't see much of Margalene in late July. Several times he walked over to her house and knocked, but was told she was resting and couldn't play. He learned she was flying often and not doing very well. When she could come out and play, they didn't do very much. They'd pick Hollyhock flowers that grew by the shed and make flower dolls. They played checkers, but he usually beat her and wasn't very good at letting her win and that made her mad. Sometimes other kids would show up and they'd play games.

Douglas's friend, David, had a bike and he was helping Doug learn to ride using his bike. It was such a big machine that Douglas could barely get on and once he got going the only way he could stop and get off was by falling over. Margalene could only watch, she wasn't allowed to ride bicycles.

"I'll ride a bike someday, you'll see," She declared with a defiant voice.

On Saturdays many of the neighbor kids would go to the movies for the afternoon matinee, mostly World War II and cowboy pictures. One day Margalene asked Douglas if he was going to see "One Hundred and One Dalmatians." He said he might but wasn't sure.

"I'd like to see it."

"Won't your folks take you?"

"Dad doesn't like kid's movies and Mom doesn't drive a car.

Douglas probably wouldn't go to see a cartoon movie about little puppies, but sensing Margalene's dejection sparked and idea. When he went home for supper, he found the newspaper and looked up show times at the theater; One Hundred and One Dalmatians was playing at 4 o'clock on Sunday afternoon. He wondered if Margalene's folks would let her go with him. It would cost fifty cents, but the yard needed mowing and he got paid fifty cents whenever he mowed it. He mowed the next morning and collected his fifty cents.

"Can I go to the movies Sunday afternoon?" He asked his mother. "I want to take Margalene to see "One Hundred and One Dalmatians." She wants to see it and her folks can't take her."

"Are you asking her out on a date?" His mom looked at him smiling. "You're pretty young to be taking girls out on dates." Mom patted him on the shoulder.

Douglas blushed but didn't say anything. He liked Margalene and wanted to take her to the movies and knew it was kind of a date and he liked that part of it as well. Even eight-year-old boys have some idea of girls as girls, so doing something a little more than playing checkers or riding on a teeter-totter had some extra appeal. The question now was will she go and will her folks let her. He now had to face the possibility of refusal. He also had to work up the courage to ask her and to get permission from her folks. It was only Wednesday, but it took him until Friday to actually get up nerve enough to cross the street prepared to ask her. Margalene was sitting on her front step and stood up as he walked over.

"Would you like to go see `One Hundred and One Dalmatians' with me on Sunday?" He blurted out, wiping his sweaty palms on his pant legs.

Her eyes widened and she put her hands up to her ears and squeezed her head.

"Oh yes, yes. I hope Mom will let me go. I'll go ask her. Margalene bolted inside. A few moments later she came back out, pulling her mother by her hand. They both sat down, side-by-side on the doorstep. Douglas stood fidgeting below on the sidewalk.

"What are you planning, Douglas?" Mrs. Johnson looked at him sternly.

"The movie is at four o'clock on Sunday. It's not too far to walk, only five blocks. It's over before six so we won't have to walk home in the dark. I've got enough money for tickets for both of us."

"You two take the cake. Douglas, you know it's a big risk letting Margalene walk that far. Who knows what can happen." She stopped and looked at Margalene and looked back at him.

He was sure she'd say no and that would be that.

"Dad will be gone Sunday, and I can't drive you. I'm so worried about letting Margalene walk that far.

"We'll go slow, and I'll hold her hand all the way." His spirits sank.

"Well, Margalene, what do you want to do?"

"Mom let me go with Doug. I'll never get to see that movie if Doug doesn't take me. Please, please.

Mrs. Johnson sat quietly, looking down at her feet. She turned to Margalene then stood up.

"Have a good time," she said and went back in the house.

"We're going to the movie," shouted Margalene.

Douglas took a deep breath trying to be as cool as an eight-year-old who just talked a girl into their first date. They discussed what time they'd leave. She said she'd bring money for treats.

Eight-year-old boys aren't very focused on girls, so Douglas didn't spend any time thinking about Sunday.

He and Dave rode Dave's bike around. Douglas and several other neighborhood boys went out to the dump north of town and looked through the trash for valuable artifacts; they didn't find any. Douglas did play baseball on Saturday and even got a hit. Sunday morning, he helped his brother deliver papers. Mostly he carried some of the papers – the Sundays are really big and heavy. They had fried chicken, sweet corn and fresh tomatoes for dinner – a favorite. Mom asked Douglas what he was going to wear to the movie. He just shrugged.

"That won't do. If you ask someone out, you've got to show them respect by looking your best. First, we're going to clean you up. Let's see your fingernails."

Mom looked at his hands, sighed and got a nail file from the bathroom. They sat in the kitchen as she cleaned and cut his fingernails.

"Go put on one of your new pairs of school pants and your new shoes. Wear a nice shirt too."

He followed Mom's directions and got dressed. Walking to the movies and back in new shoes was going to be hard on his feet but at least the shoes would be broken in for school. He went into the kitchen for Mom's inspection and approval.

"Let's go in the bathroom and comb your hair."

Cleaned, combed and polished he was ready.

"You look nice. Behave and take good care of Margalene." Mom gave him a proud smile.

As he walked across the street Margalene came out and sat down on their front step. As he got closer, she stood up and walked down to the sidewalk to meet him. She was wearing a nice dress and had two ribbons in her hair.

An eight-year-old boy and an eight-year-old girl going to a movie together doesn't generate a tremendous volume of social interaction. The pair walked hand-in-hand exchanging odd bits of conversation about likes and dislikes, things their parents did, places they've been and pets they'd owned. They sat in the third row from front of the theater. Margalene enjoyed the film very much; Douglas thought it okay. Margalene bought a bag of popcorn which they shared. Douglas walked her to the bathroom holding her hand. It fit all the attributes of a boy-girl-date but failed to generate any heart-pounding emotion. Douglas had done what he wanted to do, get Margalene to "One Hundred and One Dalmatians." They walked home and her mother invited them in for a dish of ice cream and a parental debriefing and that was that.

Late August is always dry, dusty and boring; you've done everything and are ready to go back to school. One late August afternoon, Douglas was passing the time by sitting on the Lang front step reading the "Swiss Family Robinson" when he spotted Margalene as she walked out from behind her house. He hadn't seen her for a few days, so he put down his book and ran across the street to say hello.

"We're moving. My Dad got a job in Rochester."

He didn't have much of a reaction to that news. Young kids' friendships are always transitory so having a childhood friend tell you they're leaving your life doesn't evoke strong reactions. He would miss having Margalene as a friend but had lots of other friends and there would be new friends and new faces at school in a few days. Still, he was sorry to learn she was moving away.

Margalene said they were all driving to Rochester the next day to look for a place to live and they would be gone for several days. The day the Johnsons got back Margalene and Douglas went next door and picked a couple of pears; they were ripe and sweet but kind of hard and crunchy. He held her hand both ways, but nothing happened to her.

When Douglas got home from his first day in third grade he saw a big moving van across the street; Johnsons were being loaded up and hauled away. He walked across the street to watch the loading process. The Johnsons were outside putting a few things in their car. Mrs. Johnson slid a suitcase into the trunk and turned.to Douglas.

"We'll miss you, Douglas. We'll miss this neighborhood too." She walked over and gave him a pat on the shoulder.

Margalene was next. She took his hand in hers and told him she liked him and was sad to leave.

"My dad says that they may be able to fix me in Rochester. Then I could go to a regular school and learn to ride a bike." She smiled and let go of his hand.

They got in their car and drove away. Margalene waved out the rear window to Douglas, he never saw her again.

* * *

Douglas was sitting on his deck on a balmy June Sunday morning savoring a cup of coffee and leafing through the morning paper. He glanced at an article about a woman who was retiring from her job as a pilot for a major airline. There was a picture of her dressed in her captain's uniform and sitting in the cockpit of an airliner. The article went on to say that she was one of the first woman pilots hired by that airline and became one of their first female captains. Asked about her career, she replied that she was always happiest when she was flying. The reporter asked her how she got interested in flying and she said she started flying as a youngster. She went on to say that childhood health issues made it difficult for her to get the medical certificate she needed for a pilot's license, but the doctors eventually found a heart problem that they fixed.

Douglas looked closely at the picture. She had brown eyes, and her dark eyebrows nearly met in the middle of her forehead. The caption under the photo read, "Captain Margalene Johnson retires from the cockpit after a forty-year airline flying career."

Doug smiled with satisfaction as he remembered the little girl who could fly.

Song of a Magi

Larry was late. He hopped off the forklift and started for the break room door so he could change clothes.

"Larry! Can you do me one last favor?" Bud's disembodied voice boomed from the back of the warehouse.

Larry shook his head, stopped and turned around. He'd already stayed too long doing favors for Bud. He was going to say no; but didn't want to waste time talking when he already knew that he would end up saying yes.

"Now what?"

"Just discovered a load we missed. The guy should be here any minute to pick up the trailer. It's got to be in California in three days. Can you load it? Seven boxed pallets. They're in H 3 and the trailer is at bay 7." Bud grabbed the paperwork off his desk and thrust it to Larry. "I'll sign you out for an extra half hour. And hey, there's an extra ham for you when you're finished."

"At the rate I'm going, Christmas will be over before I get out of here." Larry muttered to himself as he grabbed the papers from Bud and climbed back on the forklift, spun the wheel and headed to the pile in H 3. He loaded the truck quickly but carefully. Larry always took his time loading, even tonight. A sloppy loading job could allow the load to shift or leave the trailer unbalanced, sending the truck out of control and he didn't want that. At last, he strapped down the final pallet and quickly parked the forklift; bolting for the break room hoping to leave before Bud caught him again.

Bud had already turned off the lights in the loading dock by the time Larry walked out of the break room carrying his lunch sack and his canned ham Christmas gift. Bud tossed the extra ham to Larry, and he headed for the door.

Last year everyone got a $200 Christmas bonus check and a canned ham. This year is different, just the canned ham. Business is way down and everyone is worried but not Larry. He isn't a worrier, nothing much bothers him. He'd been laid off for nearly two weeks after Thanksgiving and had only worked half days until this week when the rush of holiday shipments got things going again. Because he was single, Larry knew they could let him go first at the next slowdown. He always saved some of his paycheck and watched his spending so a little slowdown and the prospect of getting laid off didn't bother him at all. He was hoping to get back to college in the spring semester; being laid off again would make that harder.

Still, Larry hadn't bought a single thing for Christmas. That didn't bother him much either, Christmas never was a big deal for Larry. He didn't send anyone cards, not even his folks or his brothers. As he walked to his car, Larry decided to head directly for his folks, a three-hour drive northwest of Minneapolis to New York Mills. As always, Larry had prepared carefully, his packed suitcase was in the trunk, no point in going back to his apartment either, since he'd brought extra clothes with him to work and didn't have any presents to pick up. Anyway, he was late, and he didn't want his folks to sit at the supper table wondering where he was. He tossed the two canned hams into the trunk, started his car and drove out of the parking lot.

The weather was cold and windy with just enough blowing snow to slow freeway traffic to a crawl. It took Larry almost an hour to get beyond the metro loop and onto Interstate 94. The traffic was bumper-to-bumper until he passed Clearwater. Just as he began to pick up speed, Larry caught sight of a car on the shoulder with a man in a light jacket standing next to it. Larry slowed; the car behind him honked. As Larry passed the stalled car he quickly pulled over to the shoulder, stopped and started to back up. As he did the man ran toward him and Larry stopped. Reaching Larry's car, the man opened the passenger door.

"Thank you for stopping; my car has broken." The man was shivering so hard he could hardly talk.

"Get in and shut the door," said Larry. The man slid in and pulled the door shut.

"I called for a wrecker truck, and it will be here soon. My wife and children are in the car, and they are getting very cold. Can you help us get warm again?"

Larry looked at the man, dark skinned, black haired, no gloves, light jacket and no hat. Probably from the Mideast he thought to himself. "Bring them over to my car and I'll wait till the tow truck shows up."

The man quickly herded three little girls and their mother, carrying a baby, into the Larry's car.

"My name is Hussein and my wife's name is Azra." The woman smiled and nodded. "These are my daughters Deeba, Aisha and Humaima and my son Yahya. We are most grateful."

"I'm Larry and it's nice to meet all of you." Larry smiled at the crowed back seat, and they smiled back. "Where are you headed?"

"My brother manages a motel in Fergus Falls, a Days Inn by the freeway. We're going to visit him during your holiday."

"Well, I'm headed that way. Where are they taking your car?"

"The wrecker man said to a place in the city called Waite Park. I think they will try to fix it for us."

Larry shook his head at the thought of trying to get repairs on Christmas Eve. It was already nearly six and the tow truck hadn't showed up yet.

"Well good luck with that. You may be stuck in Waite Park for a while."

Larry looked at Hussein and then turned his head toward the back and smiled at the silent and watchful faces. He fished his cell phone out of his pants pocket and rang his folks. His Mom answered.

"Is that you Larry? Are you ok?"

"I'm fine Mom, but I'm running late. I've stopped to help a guy and his family whose car broke down and we're waiting for a tow truck. I'm not quite sure how late I'll be so wait on everything. I'll call when I know more. OK?"

"Be careful. It's dark and snowing here and people drive so fast on freeways."

"I'll be fine. Talk to you later Mom. Merry Christmas! Bye."

It was only a few minutes later when a tow truck pulled up. Larry left enough room for the truck to get right in front of Hussein's car. Hussein got out and walked back to the tow truck. The driver got out and the two of them talked for a few seconds. The driver turned and walked to the back of his truck to start hooking up the disabled car. Hussein trotted back to Larry's car, pulled the door open and slid quickly in shivering.

"It's very cold. I'm glad you have a warm car for us. You're very kind. Alas I have bad news. The driver says he can only take one person with him and there are five of us. Can you help again?"

"Sure. I'll just follow the truck to Waite Park and drop you off when we get there. All of you may as well ride with me. I'll go tell the tow driver." Larry hopped out, zipped up his coat and trotted back to the tow truck driver. Larry quickly explained he'd follow behind with all of the family from the crippled car. The driver nodded, reached in his jacket pocket and pulled out a business card for the garage for Larry to use if they got separated. Larry took the card and headed quickly back to his car. With lights flashing, the tow truck pulled onto the freeway, dragging the disabled car. Larry quickly pulled out behind them.

The Halsteen Motor Service repair shop wasn't far off the freeway. The tow truck pulled up directly in front of the big door that led into the repair bays. The truck driver honked, and the big door opened, the truck pulled in and the door quickly closed. Larry parked his car next to the office door and shut off his engine.

"Let's all go inside and find out what's next."

Larry got out and everyone quickly followed; crowding through the door into a spacious office where they were greeted by a large, heavily decorated tree in a corner and a myriad of Christmas decorations. The service counter was covered with dishes of food, trays of Christmas cookies and baskets of candy. A large man wearing a Santa hat, and red coveralls emerged from the garage area and faced Larry and his passengers.

"Hi there. I'm Loren Halsteen; welcome and Merry Christmas. Not a nice way to spend Christmas Eve. Whose car do we have?" Loren smiled, put his hands on his hips and surveyed the troop.

Hussein smiled weakly and stepped forward.

"It's our car. We are going to Fergus Falls when the engine made strange sounds and then stopped. Can you repair it?"

"Well, it's like this; we stopped work at six and everyone has already left so we can't fix it tonight and we're closed tomorrow so we can't fix it then either. I'll make a couple of calls to St. Cloud if you like; just to see if there's anyone with a mechanic on duty, but they may not be able to get any parts you might need."

"What can we do? If my brother comes from Fergus Falls, he will take two hours to drive here. Where will we wait?"

"Why don't you enjoy some of our Christmas buffet while we figure out what to do." Loren waved his hand toward the loaded service counter. "My wife always makes way more food than we can possibly eat so help yourself. There's hot cider and coffee too.

The girls all look expectantly at their dad. Hussein smiled and nodded yes, adding "Be respectful and thank Mr. Halsteen."

The three girls almost in unison whispered thank you and ran to the counter.

Azra handed them each a plate. "No meat," she warned as she handed each a fork. "Only one sweet."

"Help yourself to as much as you want. Everyone's gone and I'll just have to pack up what's left and lug it home.

Larry chimed in, "Hussein, I'm headed up the interstate as far as Sauk Centre. I can take you that far and your brother can meet you there. It'll cut his drive about in half. Call him and tell him to meet us at exit 127. There's a gas station there so we'll be easy to find."

Hussein called his brother and arranged to meet at the Sauk Centre exit and described Larry's car to his brother.

"My guess is it's a broken timing belt and we should have it running by 10 AM Thursday morning. We start work a 6 AM so I can call early if we find something that'll take longer. Give me a phone number so I can call you if we're slowed up." Loren handed Hussein a pad and pen.

As Hussein wrote down his cell phone number, Loren interjected; "I've got all this food so why don't I pack it up for you to take with you. I've got plenty of plastic bags and boxes. Is that OK?"

"I'll help you box it up," said Larry.

Hussein and Azra went into the shop and returned carrying luggage, boxes and bags. Larry lifted a box of food and went out to his car where he opened the trunk. Luckily, he had lots of room.in the trunk. As Hussein and Azra loaded their possessions into the trunk, Hussein opened a large bag, searched quickly through it and retrieved a small box. There were several more trips to the office as they collected the bounty and stuffed it into the trunk.

Loren stood in the doorway and watched them leave. He smiled at the thought of telling his wife that every scrap of food, every cookie and every piece of candy had been given away to strangers in need.

The gas station at exit 127 was already closed when Larry pulled up. Their lone car stood out and would be easy to spot when Hussein's brother arrived."

Larry left the car running and turned to Hussein. "I'm glad to be able to help you. I hope the delay won't spoil your holiday."

"We are most grateful for your generosity. Our family would like to give you a gift to show that we truly appreciate what you've done." Hussein handed Larry the small box he'd taken from his luggage. "I have a small shop in Minneapolis that sells clothing favored by immigrants from many countries in Asia and Africa. Your many women friends will enjoy the beautiful scarfs that I give you to give to them. I also wish you to keep all the food that Mr. Halsteen gave us. There is a large family waiting for us in Fergus Falls and they have prepared a fine and special meal for us. We would show poor manners if we brought this food. So, will you take it please?"

Larry knew he could not refuse. Nor could he tell them that a big feast was waiting for him in New York Mills. The wait wasn't too long before a car swung off the freeway and pulled up next to them. Hussein leapt out and embraced the driver of the other car as soon as he emerged. Larry got out and unlocked his trunk and began unloading luggage and packages, pushing the food boxes aside.

Azra held Yahya under her coat as she climbed in followed by the three daughters. She clasped Larry's hand. "You are most kind and we will always thank you in our prayers."

Each of the three girls shyly shook Larry's hand. Hussein stepped close to Larry, reached out and embraced him tightly. "Peace and prosperity to you for your help. Now you go and have a Merry Christmas."

Larry watched as they drove away and then looked at his watch, shook his head and reached for his cell phone.

"Where are you?" said Larry's mother as she answered.

"I'm in Sauk Centre and I'll be there by eight thirty.

"Be careful, it's still snowing, and I think the roads are getting slippery. We'll hold supper for you.

Larry didn't think about mentioning the load of food he had in the trunk. He pulled across the freeway and headed north on Highway 71. In spite of his mother's warning, the snow was light, and the roads were dry and there was almost no traffic so he made good time. In less than forty-five minutes he was slowing for the town of Wadena where he'd turn left onto Highway 10 for the final 24 miles of his journey.

Ron Werner had planned on closing up his store, the Wadena Bottle Shop, at Six PM, but a steady stream of customers kept coming through the doors. He was alone because he'd let his only clerk go home at four. He couldn't leave the cash register to lock the door either because then there would be no way to let customers out. Finally, at Seven Thirty, there was a brief lull, so he quickly locked the front door and switched out the lights. Heaving a sigh of relief, he called his wife and said he'd be home in ten minutes. He put his cell phone down next to the cash register, pulled a bank deposit bag from under the counter, opened the register and quickly pulled the paper money out and stuffed it into the bag. Laying the bag down on the counter, he walked back to the office, grabbed his coat and pulled it on; walked back up to the front, picked up the bank bag, took out his car keys and headed for the back door.

The back door had two locks. One allowed you to open the door from the inside with a push-bar, but it was always locked so you couldn't back get in. The other lock was a dead bolt and could be locked from the outside with a key. Ron walked to the back door and reached for the handle when he realized that he'd forgotten to select some wine for the Christmas-Day dinner. He walked over to the wine section and picked out two bottles of white merlot. He was scanning the red wine section when he decided he'd need a box to carry four bottles, so he set the money bag and his car keys on the shelf and walked up to the cash register where he grabbed a small box. He quickly found a pair of red wines that suited him. He put all four bottles in the box and walked to the back door, pushed it open and stepped outside. As the door clicked shut, he realized that his car keys were on the shelf in the wine section. He muttered a soft "drat" to himself and reached into his pocked for his cell phone. The next expletive was much louder and much more vulgar than a simple "drat" as he knew that his cell phone was sitting on the counter next to the cash register.

Ron zipped up his coat and pulled on his gloves. He pondered where he might find someplace still open on Christmas Eve so he could call home and have his wife pick him up. He walked around to the front of his store and looked up and down Ash Street hoping for a glimmer of life. Every Storefront was dark; downtown was deserted and quiet. Ron now began to feel the cold and wished he'd brought a hat to work. There was a filling station on the south edge of town on Highway 71; maybe that was open he thought but it's a mile walk and probably closed already. He stood looking forlornly up and down the highway when he saw a pair of headlights coming up 71 toward him.

Larry was slowing for the stop sign where Highway 71 and highway 10 meet when a man stepped off the curb and waved a hand toward him. Larry stopped and the man ran over to the driver's side. Larry opened his window.

"Can you do me a quick favor?" Ron blurted out before Larry could even say hello. "I'm stranded with no car keys, no cell phone, no hat and there's not a single place open so I can call my wife and get a ride." Ron paused to catch his breath.

"Sure," said Larry, "get in and Merry Christmas."

Ron walked around the car and slid in and rested the wine box on his lap.

"I live just west of town a few miles. I hope that isn't too far out of your way."

"I'm on my way to New York Mills so it's no problem.

"We live on Leaf River Road just before you get to Bluffton. Boy, am I glad you came along; I got myself in a real pickle by locking myself out of my store. My wife is going to wet her pants laughing at me when she finds out what I did. Do you live in New York Mills?

"My folks live there. I'm headed home for Christmas. My brothers and their families will be over tonight and then tomorrow we'll have a big celebration at my uncle's farm near Perham."

"I've got two daughters living in Minneapolis and they're coming up tomorrow morning so we're having a quiet Christmas Eve. Probably Midnight Mass and that's it. Turn right at the Highway 75 junction and then a quick right onto Leaf River Road."

Larry made the two turns and Ron pointed out his house and Larry pulled into the driveway.

"Hey, thanks a million for helping me out. Without you, I'd be freezing my ass off in downtown Wadena. I'll tell you what; I own a liquor store, so these four bottles of wine are from my best stock. I'd like you to have them for your trouble." Ron put the box in Larry's lap. "Thanks again and Merry Christmas."

Ron got out and walked up his driveway toward his house. Larry watched for a few seconds and then backed down to the street. As he started to drive away his cell phone started to ring so he pulled his car over, stopped and got out the phone. He saw his dad's name as he answered.

"I'll bet it's you Mom. Am I right?"

"Yes. Where are you?

"I'm at Bluffton, ten minutes away. Why?

"Bad news! All of the power in town is out. It happened about half an hour ago. No one has electricity. Don Garberson, you know, the electrician; anyway, he's bringing his big generator to the church, so they'll have electricity and heat. We're all going over there now. You remember where St. Peter's Lutheran is don't you?"

"Mom, I've been there a million times, so yes, I know where it is. I should be there in fifteen minutes or so. Any idea what happened to the power?"

"I don't know. The lights went out just like that. We were wondering what to do when Mavis Wiborg called and said everyone was going to the church."

"I'll meet you there."

Larry chuckled to himself as he drove toward New York Mills. He thought about the fellowship hall; sturdy eight-foot tables, steel folding chairs, women in aprons bustling about the kitchen making coffee and everyone else standing around waiting for something to happen. "A Christmas Eve midnight smorgasbord, how Lutheran," he mused to himself."

The landmarks of the darkened town are invisible behind the veil of light snowfall. Without thinking, Larry took the cutoff onto Centennial 84 Drive and headed west. With no streetlights and all the houses dark; it seemed to Larry that he was driving into a maze with no visible clues as to where he was heading. He was just about to miss the turn onto Walker Avenue when a flashlight beam inside the fire hall caught his eye and he knew where he was. As he turned right up Walker he caught the faint glow from the church sign ahead. As he got closer, a couple pairs of headlights appeared ahead of him, groping their way toward the church. Larry followed them into the parking lot. The lot was nearly full, and the brightly lit church doorway stood out like a beacon in the darkness.

The social hall was noisy and crowded as Larry strolled in, somehow escaping notice. He spotted his parents and headed over to them where his mother smiled and grabbed him by the arm.

"Isn't this a crazy way to celebrate Christmas Eve?" She laughed and smiled.

Larry shook his head. "Do Lutherans still drink coffee? I need a cup."

Larry's mother waved to a woman wheeling a cart carrying a large metal coffee urn surrounded by a crowd of sturdy white mugs. The cart driver adroitly wheeled the cart over to Larry, filled a mug and handed it to him with a smile, then sped off toward another thirsty Lutheran.

As Larry sat down and took a small sip of his coffee Pastor Anderson's voice boomed over the PA system.

"We've got amplification! So, welcome everyone; glad you're here, indoors with electricity and heat and hot coffee and Christmas cheer. For those who aren't members of our congregation, I'm Pastor Martin Anderson and I'm so thankful that we've been able to bring light to darkness on this holy night. Thanks to everyone who helped this happen and a very special thanks to Don Garberson and his generator."

Pastor Anderson asked everyone to think about the meaning of Christmas and to be mindful of the spirit of Christmas.

"We'll pray later when the electricity comes back on and everyone can go back to their own celebrations; but, for now, let's enjoy ourselves and I want to start the fun by telling a joke."

Hajo was on his deathbed from cancer. He was so weak that they put him on the sofa in living room. He was lying there barely conscious when the smell of baking cookies took hold of him. If it is the last thing I do, he thought, I've got to have one of Minnie's cookies. He slowly slid off the sofa and crawled slowly over to the dining room table. With his last remaining strength, he reached up and picked up a cookie. He was putting it up to his mouth when Minnie yelled; "Hajo, put that back. Those cookies are for the funeral!"

The crowd laughed politely, unsure about jokes in a church on Christmas Eve,

Walter Baker called out from the back, "Here's a good one for you."

"Enno got a job bartending in Fergus Falls. The afternoon of his first day an old man comes in and sits

down at a table and tells Enno he wants three glasses of beer. Enno delivers them. The man drinks all three and leaves. The next day he comes in again and orders another three glasses of beer. Enno tells him he doesn't have to have all three at once; Enno could bring them to him one at a time. The man says he and his two brothers used to came in here every day after work for a beer. The brothers are both dead now, but he comes in and drinks their beers in their memory. One day, a few weeks later the man comes in and orders only two beers. Enno asks him why only two. The man explained; my wife made me promise to quit drinking, but she didn't say anything about my two brothers."

The crowd loosened up and the atmosphere became much more festive. Larry went out to his car and brought in the food from the garage in Waite Park. Several more men and a few women wandered to the microphone and told stories and jokes. The industrious kitchen workers rounded up the growing collection of edibles, organized them at the serving counter, set out plates and silverware and people queued up to enjoy the feast. Pastor Anderson asked everyone to join him in a prayer of thanksgiving.

After the "Amen" he smiled and continued, "today is Tuesday and you know we always have our men's beer and bible study at the Boulevard Tavern on

Tuesday nights; so, I guess it would be okay if we have a glass of wine tonight with our food. I have a bottle and a corkscrew here. If anyone else has any wine or beer, please share." He held up the corkscrew.

Larry quickly went out to his car and brought in the wine from Wadena, delivering it to the front table. He set the bottles down and he turned to go back to his table, but his way was blocked by a young woman. She was holding a bottle of wine in each hand and her eyes were twinkling merrily. Larry moved to let her pass, but she stayed put. Larry reached out to take her bottles, but she pulled them back.

"Introduce yourself first," she said mischievously.

"Merry Christmas, I'm Larry Harberts."

"Merry Christmas to you too; I'm Lorna Erickson and you don't remember me do you." She handed the two bottles of wine to Larry.

Larry remembered a much younger and plainer Lorna and never would have guessed the lovely woman standing before him was the same person.

"It's been so long, and you look much sleeker than you did the last time I saw you," he said sheepishly and blushed slightly.

"Well, don't just stand there with those two bottles of wine. Get them opened and pour me a glass of the Riesling please."

Larry threaded his way to the front tables, uncorked the two bottles of wine, poured a glass for Lorna and poured himself a glass of red. As he turned back to Lorna, he wondered what he could say to her; "Cheers and Merry Christmas" seemed too trite.

"I'm glad the power went out so we could share a glass of wine and get reacquainted." That was pretty lame he said to himself.

"Where are you living now?" Lorna asked.

"I'm up in the Cities. I live in St. Paul near highway 280 and work at a cartage company. How about you?"

"I'm pretty close to you, just south of University, close to Franklin."

"Let me take you over to say hello to my folks and then we can sit down and enjoy our wine."

Larry was hoping she'd accept his invitation. She seemed so friendly and warm he felt like he'd known her forever.

"Lead on," she said.

Larry took her hand and led her to his mom and dad. His mother recognized her at once, stood up and gave her a hug.

Are your folks here?" Larry's mom asked.

"Oh, you probably don't know; Mom had a stroke in October and she's over at Elder Home. Dad's over there now with my brother. Mom's doing okay but can't get around anymore so into the nursing home.

Dad moved in with my brother's family. They farm up by Frazee. I was at the nursing home when the power went out. Someone said that the church had power, so I came up here to say hello."

"I'm surprised I haven't heard about your mother. I'll have to get over there and say hello."

"I know she'd like that. You kind of become invisible once you're in a nursing home.

"Would you like some food?" Larry asked Lorna.

"Sure," she said. "Let's go get some." She really wasn't too hungry but wanted to talk to Larry.

They got up and walked over to the food tables where they each took a plate. Larry grabbed a handful of potato chips and a couple of cookies. Lorna went for carrot and celery sticks and a bunch of grapes.

"Are you seeing anybody?" Lorna popped a grape in her mouth.

Larry almost choked on the potato chip he'd just put in his mouth. Her question collided with the same thought he was about to blurt out. He coughed.

"No. How about you?"

"You know I've been so busy with dent tech training and being new to the cities I haven't gotten out too much."

They strolled through the crowd munching on celery sticks and potato chips until they ended back at Larry's folk's table.

"Mom. Take care of Lorna for a few minutes. I've got to go out to my car." He turned, sped off through the crowd and out the door into the parking lot. He was back quickly carrying the small box from Hussein. He sat down next to Lorna and put the box on the table.

"There is a story here," he began, "but I'm not going to tell it now. I have some special Christmas presents for you, Mom, and for you, Lorna." He opened the box and held up a pair of colorful silk scarves. One was iridescent blue and the other was shimmering gold and red and brown. He handed one to his mother and the other to Lorna.

"Give this to your mom." Larry took another scarf out of the box and handed it to Lorna. "I think I'll give one to Pastor Anderson for his wife."

Larry, now overcome with a burst of Christmas generosity, stood up, picked up the box of scarves and headed for the food table where Pastor Anderson was pouring wine. Spotting Don Garberson, Larry decided his wife needed a scarf, so he detoured and handed Don a scarf. After greeting Pastor Anderson and giving him a scarf, Larry chased down the coffee ladies and kitchen workers, handing out scarves until the box was empty. As he turned to head back to rejoin his folks, his heart sank when he saw that Lorna was no longer sitting with them. He hadn't asked her for a phone number and now wondered how he could ever reconnect. He slumped down next to his mom as his new-found Christmas Spirit vanished. He reached for a cookie as a distraction for his melancholy over his blunder. He was about to take a bite when Lorna put her hand on his shoulder. The softness of her touch sent an electric wave through his senses.

"Hey," he said. "I thought you'd left."

"I just went to say hello to some old neighbors."

Larry stood up; his Christmas spirit revived.

"Before you get away again, can I have your phone number?"

As Larry finished her request, the hall went pitch black and everyone groaned in unison.

Lorna quickly put both hands on Larry's cheeks and smothered his lips with a warm kiss. Before Larry could react, the lights came back on and everyone cheered. As Pastor Anderson announced that electricity to New York Mills had been restored Larry put his arm around Lorna and returned her kiss.

Everyone scrambled to pack up and get to their cars. Larry and Lorna exchanged phone numbers. Lorna invited Larry to join her for New Year's Eve; Larry accepted. They strolled casually hand in hand to Lorna's car.

Large downy snowflakes floated serenely earthward to accentuate the tranquil tradition of

Christmas Eve. Larry and Lorna shared a parting kiss; each believing that their chance encounter was a true gift of Christmas.

A Message from Marcel

"I'm going for a short walk," Marge shouted toward me as she went out the door. I didn't even look up from my laptop as she left; I still regret not looking up.

My memories of the rest of that day are lost in a swirling, foggy blur. A policeman appears and summons me, a swift ride to the hospital. Gurneys, surgeons, nurses, frantic action and finally stillness and all I can see is Marge, swathed in white, her head, now shaved and wrapped in bandages. A car jumped the curb the policeman said. In that awful moment my loving wife flew away forever to be followed by three days of chaos. Burying your life's partner is like falling down a steep rocky hillside for three long days. Then it's over and you're at the bottom, alone in the dark, bruised, torn and not knowing what to do next.

Our two sons stayed with me for a couple of extra days. Doug, the oldest, did the "outside" work. He went to the bank and made sure his mom's accounts were closed, he rolled all of her retirement funds into mine, he worked with the funeral director to get death certificates to everyone that needed them. After two days of his efforts, the living Marge was gone, wiped away.

Steve stayed "inside" and shepherded me through the survivor's tasks. We waded through all the sympathy cards and I wrote thank you notes while Steve addressed the envelopes. Together we drove to neighbors and friends returning dishes and cake pans. On the second evening we had a pizza delivered and the three of us sat, mostly silent, as we ate mechanically with much-needed glasses of wine. The next morning, we took a small, plain wooden box holding all that was left of Marge to the cemetery. The headstone Marge and I had ordered when we picked out our plot had already been placed and Steve had arranged for a small hole just in front of it. The three of us walked together from the car to the plot; I carried Marge. We all knelt down as I placed the box into the hole. No one said anything; the week had drained us of all the goodbyes and farewell prayers. After the boys filled the hole with a shovel left there for us, I laid a bouquet of red, pink, white and yellow roses on top of the mound. We all stood sorrowfully silent for a few moments and then turned away and trudged back to the car. That afternoon Doug and Steve hugged me, said tearful farewells and left to resume their lives.

I remained behind, suspended in the empty fog of loneliness. Depression held me in a strange prison, unable to move, paralyzed, my mind a blank, except for mournful thoughts of Marge. I desperately needed something to reawaken me, to bring color back into my life, to help me overcome the despair I'd sunk into. In a desperate attempt to shake off my lethargy I registered for an international conference on telecommunication security protocols. A week in Paris at the beginning of May should lift my spirits. The timing of the conference would give me a couple of weeks to make travel arrangements and time enough to let my clients know I'd be gone for an extra week.

Flying from Minneapolis to Paris didn't seem like a particularly arduous journey; Leave Minneapolis in early afternoon, land in Boston for a few hours, depart for Paris in early evening, enjoy a sunset supper over the Atlantic and sleep until sunup over France. However, the confined idleness on the plane served only to deepen my depression as I sat, longing to have Marge beside me. I imagined we were discussing the places we'd visit that we'd skipped our last time in Paris. I ached to have her in the seat next to me.

Unlike Marge, I never had much trouble sleeping on long night-flights, but now I slept fitfully, dreamily yet not dreaming. Marge and Paris kept intruding into my slumber. Traveling Business Class with more comfortable space didn't help me much. I fidgeted and shifted and pulled at my blanket and rearranged my pillow but still sleep evaded me. I began to think this trip was a bad idea. Finally, dawn arrived to rescue me from my wearying wrestling match with Morpheus. All I remember about breakfast was the coffee. I gulped several cups before I began to feel any anticipation for my sojourn in Paris.

The journey is completed by a wildly exciting cab ride from Charles de Gaulle Airport into the heart of Paris. Parisian traffic is always lively as drivers substitute verve and élan for rules and caution and my taxi driver was no exception. He weaved from lane to lane with abandon, gestured menacingly to other drivers doing the same. The cab journey was thrilling and terrorizing, punctuated by gasps and involuntary recoils from near misses. A taxi ride is the perfect way to start a stay in the City of Lights. By the time we stopped at my hotel I was wide awake and eager for emersion into the distractions of the city.

It is impossible to explain but I've always felt that I belonged in this city. When I'm here I feel at ease and alert, the sounds, smells, traffic, passers-by, cafés and voices surround me with a blanket of soothing lightness. Everything seems to go better when I'm in Paris. I needed something to go better!

Alas, Marge would not go away. She drifted before my eyes and whispered into my thoughts. After checking in I could barely wait to escape the emptiness of my hotel room, if only she were there in the flesh. I quickly rifled through my carryon, grabbed my conference registration packet, bolted for the elevator and escaped. After I dropped my room key at the front desk I rushed outside and hailed a taxi to the conference center. To my surprise, it was only a few blocks away, close enough to walk and enjoy the bustling boulevards.

I was not disappointed by the conference. It was worthwhile and the hospitality was wonderful. Best of all, I was distracted enough to leave Marge out of my thoughts most of each day. I enjoyed meeting old friends as well as making new ones. Eating lunch and dinner in large groups and engaging in spirited discussions perked me up. I was distracted and had more energy but was still melancholy.

The conference ended early on the last day, and my return flight didn't leave until the next morning so I set out on foot to enjoy a long afternoon of freedom; I hoped a stroll on the boulevards along the Seine would cheer me up. A late morning rain cooled and scrubbed Paris and now the afternoon light bathed the city in that almost heavenly radiance unique to the City of Lights. I took the Metro to the Hotel de Ville station and wound my way down Rue St. Bon across the Seine onto Isle de la Cité at Pont Notre Dame. The Cathedral is always a crowded madhouse, so I didn't stop there and instead headed directly across the island for the Petit Pont. My quick walk left me somewhat winded so I stopped on the bridge. I leaned over the railing and gazed down at the Seine. As I gazed down at the river Marge crept back into my thoughts. How I longed to put my arm around her and talk about our time together.

"Si vous sautez, vous mourrez."[1]

The woman's voice startled me enough to make me jerk up! I couldn't help but smile as I turned and got a look at her. Many Parisian women radiate a certain commanding presence as if they are the royal princesses of the boulevard; they stride purposefully, erect with their shoulders back and their head held high. She stood there, the embodiment of the boulevard princess, hands on her hips looking at me intently waiting for a response.

"Le chat a-t-il ta langue?" [2]

I shook my head and spoke one of the few French phrases I knew. "Parlez anglais s'il vous plaît."

The woman laughed and waved her hands in the air. "You're American! Why do you want to end your

____

[1] If you jump; you will die!
[2] Has a cat got your tongue.

life in the Seine? If you survive your leap the water will infect you and you will become sick and die anyway."

"I was just looking at the river and wondering where I should go from here," I lied with a short laugh. The truth was I wondered what death was like and if drowning was agony or peace. What made her guess my thoughts?

The woman was probably about my age, maybe forty or so but she looked younger; somehow, most women in Paris look younger. She was tall, slim with long brown hair and bright grey eyes. I glanced at her feet, high heels but no stockings; Parisian women of this stature never wear hose or stockings it seems.

I smiled at her but was curious about how she was dressed. Her shoes were heavy looking with squat heels. Her outfit, a jacket and skirt were light gray, looked expensive but seemed dated. Something about her seemed odd but I couldn't quite figure out why. Maybe it was the hat, also gray with a large floppy brim. Women don't often wear hats anymore I thought. I was about to try to start a conversation when she cut me short.

"I'm happy that you are not going to jump into the Seine. You won't find what you are looking for by staring into the water. Find new love and you will again be happy. Enjoy Paris." With that declaration, she smiled, strode by and marched triumphantly across the bridge and into the crowd around Notre Dame Cathedral.

I watched her go with a tinge of sadness at a missed opportunity to learn more about her. Energized by meeting her, I decided I needed a coffee so I walked across the Quai St. Michel and headed down Quai de Montebello for the sidewalk café next to the Shakespeare & Co. Bookstore. The café' is busy and there are no empty tables. A waiter saw me looking for a place and walked over toward me. He pointed to a table with an old man and an empty chair. I nodded and wound my way to the empty chair. The old man smiled as I motioned to the seat.

"Parlez vous anglias?" I asked

"A Bit."

"May I sit with you while I enjoy a coffee?"

"You are most welcome. My name is Marcel." He held out his hand.

"Merci. My name is Gordon." I shook his hand and sat down.

I signaled the waiter. "Café au lait s'il vous plaît," I asked. Americans insist on frothing café au lait and calling it latté but I've always preferred the French version, espresso and steamed milk only, no foam.

I sat contentedly, waiting for my coffee while eyeing the park just across from the Square Rene' Viviani. Next to the square is the ancient church St. Julien-Le-Pauvre.

"Are you American?" Marcel asked.

"Yes."

"Have you been to this place before?"

"Yes, my wife and I used to always stop here for coffee whenever we came to Paris."

The waiter brought my coffee and Marcel signaled he wanted another of whatever he was drinking.

I took a sip of my coffee and waited.

"Your wife was not allowed to accompany you this time?" Marcel looked at me with a somewhat sorrowful expression on his face.

I looked down, shook my head slowly and then looked at Marcel.

"She's with me in memory." I pointed to my head and gave a slight smile.

"I'm sorry for you and sorry for asking." He raised his hand apologetically.

We sat in silence for a few minutes.

"Do you come here often?" I decided to see if I could restart our conversation.

 "Yes. I live nearby. This café is pleasant, and I enjoy watching the tourists. This is a very inhabituelle place. I'm sorry for the French but the English word will not come. Perhaps `peculiar' is close.
Ah, now it comes to me, `unusual'. If you sit here awhile you might see unusual things."

I could only smile because what he said didn't make any sense to me. I must have looked puzzled because he put his hand on my arm and leaned forward.

"This is one of the oldest places in Paris. Church St Julian across the boulevard, was built in the thirteenth century but it replaced a Merovingian church built in the sixth century. This place has seen much over the centuries and many people, including me, believe that there are unexplained things that happen here." Marcel took a sip of his drink and leaned back in his chair and smiled.

"Like what?" I asked.

"During the last war this café was used by the Resistance as a place to pass messages, but because everyone was being watched they couldn't meet one another, or they'd be spotted and caught so they used the waiters. A man would arrive and sit at a table by himself. The waiter would approach and take his order. When the waiter returned the man would pass a slip of paper and tell the waiter who to pass it to. When the recipient arrived, the waiter would pass the message. It was a dangerous game, and many were caught. There was a well-known fashionable woman, Liselotte Guyot was her name. She came to this very Café every day for déjeuner[3] with her friends. She was a courier for the La Résistance. The Bosch would not suspect a elegant lady to be involved in such dangerous activities.

She was very clever but so were the colaborators who spied on everyone. One afternoon, as she stood up to leave her friends, a car pulled up and three men jumped out. They tried to grab Liselotte but she alluded their grasp and ran toward the square. One of the men drew a pistol and shot her. She fell in the

---

[3] Luncheon

street and died there. I was very young, only six years old but I remember the day. Liselotte was my mother."

Marcel closed his eyes and shook his head slowly.

"I think she ran so they would kill her there. If she was captured, they would find ways to make her tell what she knew and many others would die. I have always believed that."

I had no voice; I just sat there dumbstruck by his story. He took another sip of his drink, smiled at me and turned, looking toward the street for a moment. He turned back and smiled at me.

"Now I will tell another unusual happening here. Some people say there is a woman who walks these streets and greets strangers. I've never seen her but I'm sure she's here. She is described as well dressed in a gray suit with a large gray hat. Those who claim to have seen her say she always gives them a message of hope."

I started to tell him of my encounter but couldn't speak. At last, I was only able to mutter "a lame `amazing story."

Marcel stood up ready to leave. He surveyed the crowded café and then turned back to me. "My mother often wore a gray suit and hat. I remember seeing how wonderful she looked in that jacket and dress. I like to think she still wears it." He paused and reached out for my hand.

"Gordon, it is my pleasure to meet and talk to you."

I grasped his hand as he held mine in a firm grip.

"I hope the stories of an old man didn't make you think I am becoming senile. Anyway, enjoy the rest of your stay. Au revoir." He gave a small wave as he walked away.

I finished my café au lait and looked at the people seated around me, wondering why the waiter sent me to sit with the old man. Did he know that Marcel was there to pass a message to me?

Time has passed and Marge still comes to me often; though memory encounters of her are now happier ones. I have returned again to Paris and again enjoyed a café au lait at the café by the Shakespeare & Company bookstore. The crowds at Notre Dame are even larger now with gawkers looking at the fire-ravaged cathedral. After I finished my coffee I walked across the Petite Pont, stopped and stared down at the Seine. As I looked over the railing at the dark water I smiled and thought of Liselotte and Marcel. Neither of them appeared.

Silver

Dennis shut his eyes as anger welled up in him. Jack wouldn't stop pushing, insisting that Dennis was the only one who could do it. The argument had lasted for way too long and Dennis couldn't think of any way to break the logjam and escape.

"Come on Denny. It's only a box of silverware. Just take it and we'll be done with this. Why are you being so stubborn?" Jack pushed the wooden chest across the table toward Denny.

The four Jacobson siblings were spending the morning at their parent's home sorting through what was left after the estate sale. Their father, John, had slipped away quietly one night over a year ago. John never wanted to be a burden to anyone so it seemed proper for him to simply stop breathing and depart without causing any fuss. Helen carried on well after losing John. She entertained friends, played bridge, visited her children and worked at her crafts. Almost a year passed before she called her daughter Catherine.

"I want to invite the four of you and your spouses to dinner next Sunday; if that works for everyone," she informed Catherine. "I'll make roast beef and mashed potatoes; can you have everyone else bring something? Ask Dennis to bring some wine; he knows what everyone likes."

Catherine talked to her mother for a while but never got a clear picture of her mom's intentions. She guessed maybe Helen wanted to sell the house and move into an apartment. That made sense Catherine thought. The three boys shared the upkeep chores so Helen didn't have any reason to move except basement steps for laundry and they'd already made plans to relocate the washer and dryer into the pantry off the kitchen. Catherine shrugged it off and called her brothers to set up the dinner.

There hadn't been a real family dinner since before John died so everyone arrived in a festive mood. The mid-August weather was just perfect so they all crowded around the picnic table on the deck for wine and hors d'oeuvres. They probably would have stayed outside to eat but Helen had already set the dining room table.

"Let's go inside before everything gets cold." Cathy started herding everyone indoors.

The dinner conversation never slowed down enough for anyone to ask why their mother invited them over. Finally, as Jack's wife, Donna, handed out slices of her delicious pecan pie topped with French Vanilla ice cream Michael held up his dessert fork, waved at his mother and asked, "Ok Mom, what's your excuse?"

"I have a story to tell." Helen paused and smiled. "Two weeks ago, I started seeing strange lights and colors and I began to have lingering headaches and I never have headaches. So, I made a doctor's appointment. They gave me an MRI and found a brain tumor."

The festive mood whooshed out of the room like a bursting balloon. Everyone sat in stunned silence.

Before anyone could speak Helen continued. "There's more; the next day I visited a specialist and had some tests done. I have a fast-growing cancerous tumor that's inoperable. There are treatments but not very promising so I've decided not to have any."

"Oh Mom!" Catherine stood up and ran to her mom wrapping her arms around her.

"Please sit down and let me finish my story." Helen waved Catherine back to her seat.

"For now, I'm staying here. Ruth Anderson and her cat are coming over to live with me; I can't really be alone anymore. The bad thing about brain tumors, like the one I have, is that no one can predict what will happen. So, I can't drive anymore and I can't be alone either. Ruth has a car so you guys won't have to haul me around. Right now, I'm fine except for strange vision events and headaches."

"What can we do?" Michael asked. "There must be something; some kind treatment."

"I don't think I can escape and I don't want to try. I'll stay right here as long as I can and then go to hospice.

The tumor quickly consumed Helen. Her eyesight left first then her balance. She never made it to hospice. By late September, the day before she was to be moved to hospice, Ruth discovered Helen peacefully at rest.

As Jack pushed the silverware chest across the table Dennis stood up, went over to the sliding patio door and stepped outside into the bright October sunshine. He was trembling with anger. As he stood brooding, he felt a slight tug at his sleeve and looked over to see Catherine standing next to him. He just glowered at her.

"Can I tell you something?" Catherine took his hand.

Dennis smiled wanly and nodded his head.

"When I was nine my friend Mary called me up one Saturday morning and asked if I'd liked to come over and listen to her records. She'd bought a couple of new ones I hadn't heard before. I grabbed my coat and headed for the back door. Mom was just coming up the basement steps with a load of laundry and she asked me to take them outside and hang them up. Dennis, I just exploded! I got so angry so quickly! I yelled at Mom. `Am I the only one who ever gets told to help? Can't I go anywhere without you grabbing me with chores to do?' Mom dropped the laundry basket and grabbed me by the arm, hauled me over to the kitchen table, pulled out a chair, sat down and pulled me over. I thought she was going to spank me! Then she put her arms around me and gave me a hug and then she started kissing me and running her hand over my cheek and whispering that she loved me and was sorry for stopping me and asking me to hang up clothes. My anger just melted away. I was ashamed and felt selfish for not helping. I hugged her and kissed her and went over, picked up the laundry basket and went outside and hung everything up."

Catherine smiled at Dennis, stood up, took him by the hand and led him back inside.

The two of them sat down and Dennis opened the silverware chest.

"I have an idea. Let's divide the silver into four sets. We can each take our pieces home and when we get together on Christmas or Thanksgiving, we can get them out and use them."

Everyone seemed to accept the suggestion and Dennis carefully divided up the knives, forks, salad forks and teaspoons. He separated the gravy ladle, butter knife, slotted spoon and serving spoon, putting one of them on each pile.

"I'll give the chest to the Salvation Army. I'm hauling the picnic table over there tomorrow anyway."

Everyone pocketed their silverware and stood up to leave. They edged slowly toward the front door looking fondly around the nearly empty living room. The few remaining sticks of furniture will be gone by tomorrow and their connection to the house would be erased.

Arlouine was sitting at the kitchen table drinking a cup of coffee when Dennis walked in.

"How'd everything go?"

"We fought over the good silver. Nobody wanted to take it. I suggested we split it up four ways so that's what we did."

Dennis took the silverware pieces out of his jacket pocket and laid them on the table.

"Do you want some coffee?"

"Yes, thanks. I think I'll polish this stuff before I put it away."

Dennis walked over to the cupboard and searched through the top shelf until he found the silver polish.

Arlouine poured him a cup of coffee as he pulled a rag from under the sink, wet it and sat down across the table next to his coffee. He carefully polished each piece of silverware. When he finished, he carried the silver to the sink where he washed each piece in soapy water, rinsed and dried them. He then carried the now shining silverware back to the table and spread everything out in a gleaming row.

"Well," said Arlouine, "They look nice but what will we do with a three-piece set of silverware?"

"We decided that whenever we get together for a meal, everyone will bring their silver and we'll reassemble the full set. I guess that will work."

Dennis got up and went to the dishtowel drawer. He rummaged around a bit, pulled out a towel, walked back to the table, sat down, spread the towel out and carefully grouped the pieces together. He then folded the towel over the entire collection and rolled it up.

"OK, where do you want it?"

Arlouine looked at Dennis and smiled wickedly. "You're not going to get away with making me find the spot to store your stash. You brought em home you figure out where to put em. I suggest your sock drawer."

Dennis just smiled. "I'll think of a place don't worry."

"Watching you polish the silver made me think of one of the last times your mom came over. We were sitting here at the table having coffee when she told me a story about what happened to her and Catherine.

"You were still pretty small then, maybe seven or eight. Helen said she was bringing up a load of laundry one Saturday morning when Catherine walked through the kitchen saying she was going to a friend's house. Helen said she just lost her temper at Catherine for leaving and not helping. Then, Helen told me, a strange thing happened. As she grabbed Catherine's arm to stop her and scold her for leaving without helping the anger suddenly vanished and a powerful surge of love swept over her. Helen said she sat down, pulled Catherine onto her lap and hugged and kissed her and told her over and over how much she loved her. She cried as she hugged and kissed Catherine. At first, Catherine squirmed, trying to escape and then her mother's love infected her, she relaxed and put her arms around her mother and nestled her head on her mother's shoulder. Helen paused and told me she started to cry. Helen said she watched Catherine stand up, put on her coat and pick up the laundry basket. 'I've got it Mom,' she said to me. I just sat there and watched her go. I was sitting there in kind of a trance when John came from whatever he was doing in the garage; as he walked by I grabbed his arm and told him `don't take off your jacket, we're going downtown to buy a clothes dryer.' I've never forgotten that overwhelming burst of love that swept over me. I still feel it whenever I look at the four of them and I don't think I ever was able to get angry at them either."

Arlouine looked at Dennis and smiled. "Your Mom was an angel. Why don't you put that silverware in the box with ours; I'm sure they will fit just fine."

Dennis smiled back at Arlouine. He didn't let on that Cathy had also told him the story. He took a sip of his coffee and thought about the story twice-told. "What's for supper?" He blurted out.

"Goulash."

"Will there be enough for four?"

"I guess so; why?"

"I'm going to ask Jack and Doris over. Maybe we can play cards or something."

Dancing on the Moonlight

DAY 1

Rosemary sighed and shook her head as she walked out the door and into the hall. There was no pleasing Amber Hallerman. Rosemary had been the nurse supervisor at Open Arms for twelve years and thought she was pretty tough; but she didn't know how much longer she could take Amber's abuse. The old lady and her mean-spirited antics made Rosemary's job wearing and wearying.

"Don't you dare walk out on me you cruel witch." There was a loud thump as a book landed on the floor. "Pick up my book!" Amber pulled the cord on the call switch above her bed and threw off her blanket and sheet.

Rosemary stopped, took a breath, thought about yelling back, "pick it up yourself you old battle axe." Relieved by her unuttered thought, she looked up the hall for help and saw Gloria pushing a wheelchair toward her. With her most sympathetic smile she beckoned to Gloria.

Gloria answered before Rosemary could speak.

"I know, I know. Amber's awake and mad as hell at everyone and everything and it's my turn to get her to breakfast. I'm a forty-three-year-old black woman," Gloria said to no one in particular as she strode past Rosemary, "changing diapers and wiping bottoms for twelve dollars an hour. My reward must be in heaven because it sure as hell isn't here at Open Arms." Gloria winked at Rosemary, put on a brave smile and walked to Amber's doorway.

"You're late and you're slovenly and I want my breakfast." Amber struggled to sit upright. Amber Hallerman is seventy-nine but still handsome and trim, with intense blue eyes and hair that is just now turning from steel-grey to white. She'd had a mild stoke three months ago that left her unable to keep her balance. She'd tried to get by with a walker but after several falls a county social worker called and said she'd have to move from her apartment into a facility that could, as the social worker put it, "meet your needs." Amber didn't like the idea but didn't protest, living alone had become frightening, particularly at night when she couldn't orient herself in the dark. The move to Open Arms was made easily and she adapted quickly, and everything seemed to go well for the first few days.

Slowly though, Amber began to change. Anger surfaced easily in her and it slowly took over until she was soon battling with everyone who came near her. The cause of this change in her behavior seemed to be related to her stroke but remained unexplained, even Amber didn't know why she was angry.

Rosemary headed back down the hall to her office. She could see a woman seated in front of her desk. Rosemary knew she had an appointment with the mother of young girl who was arriving the next day. The girl, Rebecca Russell, represented a new challenge for Rosemary, a challenge that Rosemary hoped would help her cope with Amber.

"Hello," said Rosemary as she entered. "I hope I didn't keep you waiting too long. You must be Sharon Russell?"

"Good morning. Yes, I'm Sharon, Rebecca's mother."

Sharon stood up and held out her hand. Rosemary reached out and put both her hands around Sharon's, holding tight but not squeezing.

"Oh my," said Rosemary, "you've got nice warm hands. Nurses love warm hands. I'm Rosemary Dolan, Director of Nursing here at Open Arms. Please sit down. We've got a lot to talk about." Rosemary let go of Sharon's hand, pulled a chair away from the wall and sat down in front of her desk, next to Sharon.

"Would you like some coffee or tea? Be not afraid, our cooks are without peer and their coffee is as good any and we've got every tea you might like. I'm going for the coffee; how about you?"

Sharon nodded. "I like cream, if it's not too much trouble."

Rosemary reached over her desk, picked up her phone and asked the front desk to have an aide bring in a pot of coffee and two cups.

"Now, let's get acquainted. I've read the medicals on your daughter, so I already know a lot about her condition. What do you want me to know?"

Sharon took a deep breath, looked at the floor and was relieved when the Gloria arrived with the coffee. Sharon waited while Rosemary poured them each a cup, stirred in some cream, took a sip and set the cup down.

"I'm kind of lost. Rebecca is so close but so far away. I can feel her, talk to her and look at her but don't know where she is. I'm afraid she'll never come back."

Sharon described the awful accident. A driver fell asleep. Rebecca's best friend tried to steer away but couldn't. Rebecca was so mangled and broken that no one offered much encouragement. As the days slid along, Rebecca's body slowly mended. The bones and screws and plates and wires gradually solidified, the surgeons repaired and rebuilt and at last the body healed. Rebecca, however, remained suspended, silent, blank. The accident was two months ago, and Rebecca shows few signs of awakening. Oh, there are days when her blood pressure rises and her temperature goes up close to normal, her heart beats a little faster and she seems to be more alert. The intensive care nurses would hover expectantly, talk soothingly, and rub her hands, anything to stimulate arousal. Then she would slowly retreat into the quiet abyss.

"You know the rest. They've done everything at the hospital, there's no reason for her to be there anymore. Now all we can do is wait and hope." Sharon smiled weakly at Rosemary and took another sip of coffee.

"I can't say I understand how you feel because you have to live it to understand it, but I know that we'll do everything we can to support you." Rosemary sat up a little straighter and looked carefully at Sharon. "Now I need your help. Rebecca will be sharing a room with a woman named Amber Hallerman. Let's go meet her and let you take a look at the room. You need to know that Amber can be very abrasive; you'll see what I mean. I'll explain as we go."

Rosemary described the previous attempts to fill the other bed on Amber's room. Each had failed quickly. Amber just wouldn't let up. Her constant harangue wore the staff and the roommate down and within a few days, Amber was alone again. Medicare payments required Amber to be in a double room and Open Arms couldn't leave a bed vacant just because she didn't want anyone next to her. Amber's behavior was Rosemary's problem and Rosemary desperately hoped that Amber would accept Rebecca. She knew Rebecca wouldn't be a problem and she hoped Sharon would be able to put up with Amber.

Rosemary and Sharon arrived at Amber's room just as Amber's wheelchair reached her doorway.

"Amber, this is Sharon Russell. Sharon's daughter is coming to live with us and she's going to share your room." Rosemary smiled at Amber and then looked at Sharon.

"It's nice to meet you." Sharon held out her hand, reached toward Amber and smiled.

Uncharacteristically, Amber was silent but only for a moment. "Hello. My breakfast is getting cold. Get out of my way. Gloria, push me."

Gloria shrugged, nodded at Sharon and shook her head as she and Amber wheeled through the door.

"Oh my, I see what you mean."

Rosemary stood by as Sharon surveyed the room. Amber's bed was nearer the door and Rebecca's would be under the window; Sharon liked that. A sliding panel could be extended to give each occupant a measure of privacy. Two dressers lined the opposite wall, and a comfortable chair sat next to each bed.

"A little less institutional than the hospital, but still not very homey. Hard to make a nursing home anything else I guess." Sharon turned to Rosemary with a slightly downcast look.

"You're right. I know it doesn't change things, but we refer to Open Arms as a residential facility not a nursing home. Let's go talk to the physical therapist about Rebecca."

DAY 2

Elizabeth Fredrick always made a point of stopping by Rosemary's office whenever she came to visit her mother. Today, seeing the office empty she simply signed the visitor's log, clipped on a pink visitor's badge and headed straight for her mother's room. Elizabeth was worried about her mother's anger and abusiveness; it was so unlike her to treat everyone as though they were her enemies. She'd even snapped at Elizabeth on her last visit. Elizabeth opened the door. Amber was sitting in her chair. On seeing her daughter, she simply raised her hand in greeting, her face expressionless.

"Hi Mom. I brought you a book of poems I bought." Elizabeth reached over, took her mother's hand and laid the book in her lap.

Amber, smiling weakly, picked up the book. "Poetry, thank God, you brought me some new poetry. There's no poetry here. I can't breathe here. I'm surrounded by imbeciles." Amber suddenly stopped and looked at Elizabeth. "Oh Lizzy, I'm Sorry. I can't help myself anymore. When I'm sleeping, I dream angry dreams. Everyone hates me now."

"Mom, I love you and I wish there was a way I could take you with me and make you happy again."

"I know you would if you could. Let's not talk about that." Amber picked up the book and opened it to the table of contents. "New names. All women. Katriana Deverroux, Gwendolyn Golden, all new names. This should be fun to read."

Elizabeth was relieved to see her mother relaxed and at ease. She felt guilty about her inability to care for her at home but there were too many barriers.

"They're moving a girl in here this afternoon. This place will be a zoo. People running in and out. No privacy, nothing but trouble. You've got to do something."

"Mother, what has come over you? Why are you so angry at everyone? They're trying their best to help you."

Amber looked out the window, her lips were moving, but she was silent. Elizabeth, close to tears, started to get up, thinking of just leaving.

"Hello." Sharon Russell stood in the doorway with a vase full of flowers in one hand clutching a cloth bag with the other. "I'm bringing some things for Rebecca, may I come in?"

Elizabeth stood up and smiled in relief at the interruption. "Hi, I'm Elizabeth Fredrick and this is my mother, Amber Hallerman. Let me help you with those flowers."

"Amber and I have met, sort of. Nice to see you again." Sharon smiled at Amber. Amber gave a slight nod, her face stoically expressionless.

"They'll be bringing Rebecca in a few minutes. I'm sorry for all the commotion, but things will quiet down after she gets settled.

Amber gave a slight but audible "humph."

Sharon was right. Within minutes Gloria strode into the room and pulled down the covers on Rebecca's bed. As she completed her task, two EMTs wheeled in a gurney carrying Rebecca. The three of them eased Rebecca off the gurney and onto her bed. Elizabeth and Amber, trapped by the gurney, were crowded into the corner by the door. Elizabeth began plotting an escape and tried to catch Gloria's eye without causing too much more commotion. At that moment,

Rosemary walked in, looked at Amber and Elizabeth, and said she'd be right back. Within Seconds she was back with a wheelchair.

"There's coffee and cookies in the Sunroom, let's take a break. Come on you two." She reached over and helped Amber into the wheelchair. Amber didn't protest and Elizabeth smiled thankfully.

Amber was right; having Rebecca in the next bed was a zoo! Caring for a comatose person is an active process. There's the feeding tube so meals, such as they are, and water are brought in and administered. Her physical needs require changing diapers, pajamas and bed clothes. Twice every day the staff wheeled in a "lift" that they used to move Rebecca into a reclining chair for the trip to physical therapy. The commotion was constant. Amber now spent most of her day in the Sunroom reading or playing solitaire. She was unusually quiet, but everyone gave her a wide berth, careful not to get in her line of fire.

DAY 3

"What do you want?" Barked Amber!

Doctor Schade, startled by the harsh query, stepped back and looked at the name plates on the door to make sure he had the right room. "I'm here to see Rebecca Russell. Sorry for the intrusion. I'm Doctor

Schade and I'll be coming to see Rebecca often for the next few weeks. I won't cause much of a fuss."

Amber eyed him with a mixture of suspicion and hostility from her chair by her bed. "That's fine," she said. "Will you talk to me?" Her query was as much a command as it was a question. "This young girl was shoved into this room, and nobody has the decency to introduce us let alone tell me anything about her. You'd think I was just a lump of coal."

Dr. Schade looked at Rebecca, then looked at his watch then looked at Amber. "First, I'd like to examine Rebecca then I would very much like to talk to you because I need your help. Fair enough?"

Amber sat back in her chair, opened the book she was reading. "Yes," she replied. "I'll wait."

Dr. Schade spent far more time with Amber than he should have, but he sensed that Amber needed to understand the girl in the next bed. Explaining Rebecca's condition almost requires a complete medical lecture on comas, how they're caused, how they affect the person, how they're treated and if you ever recover. Amber remained silent throughout Dr. Schade's explanation.

"Will she ever get better?"

"All I can tell you is that after two months, the chances are becoming slimmer, but we don't really know. She could already be aware of what's going on around her but unable to move or speak."

"Can she hear us?"

"Maybe. There is a husband-and-wife team, the Mindells, who have developed a technique called `Process Therapy' that works with whatever minimal response a patient exhibits as a way of helping the patient to communicate. If we can find some response from Rebecca, we'll use that therapy."

"Does she have brain damage?"

"As I said earlier, we've done CT scans, and everything looks normal. Her brain wave activity looks normal too. Being awake or asleep is controlled by a part of the brain called the `reticular formation' and that seems to be keeping Rebecca asleep."

"Does she Dream?"

Dr. Schade laughed at the question. "I'll answer that the next time I'm here. Now I have to get back to the clinic. Remember what I asked; if you see or hear anything that you think is important, no matter how small, let me know when I come in." He gave Amber's hand a soft squeeze, stood up, pushed his chair back to Rebecca's bedside and strode out.

DAY 6

Rosemary saw Amber seated in the corner of the Sunroom seemingly engrossed in a book. Looking a little closer, Rosemary decided that Amber was sleeping. The sight of Amber sleeping caused Rosemary to ponder Amber's behavior over the past few days. There had been far fewer outbursts, and the harsh language seemed to have softened at little. Maybe, Rosemary mused, Amber is feeling more at home. She made a mental note to ask more detailed questions about her at Amber's next assessment review.

Amber hadn't made any friends among the residents at Open Arms. Wanda Rienstra was an interesting woman who read and understood poetry. Wanda was very, very old and frail and within a few days after they met, Wanda no longer appeared in the Sunroom. Amber guessed that Wanda had "moved on." At meals, Amber often sat with Miriam Anderson. Miriam was younger than Amber and was alert and talkative. Miriam had a short-term memory deficiency. Sometimes Amber had to help Miriam eat because Miriam would forget what she was doing.

Amber disliked mealtimes. The food was, as she put it, "industrial." The dining room was too bright and bland, too noisy and crowded and worst of all, she had to sit in line in that damned wheelchair and wait to be wheeled into the dining room like a complete invalid. She begged her aide to let her try to use a walker. The answer was always "No!" They said if she fell, they'd be in trouble with the State. "They won't be happy until I sit there in my nightgown and bib, drooling with the rest of the vegetables." She called Elizabeth more often than she should and begged her to take her out for Chinese or Mexican and a cocktail.

DAY 8

Gloria was working a double shift, six A.M. to Midnight. Whenever someone couldn't make the swing shift Gloria usually volunteered. She always needed the extra pay. Though usually dead tired after a full day, Gloria didn't mind working nights; the visitors were all gone, by 9 o'clock the residents were in their rooms, and most were asleep. The hall lights were dimmed, and everyone's door was left open to make it easier to check for problems. Gloria spent most of her night shift checking on resident's rooms and answering call lights, most of which were for simple requests.

At eleven o'clock she got up from her chair behind the control desk and started her rounds, walking slowly down each hallway, stopping at each door for a moment, looking at each bed, listening for any unusual sounds. As she approached Amber and Rebecca's room she heard a soft voice. When she got to the doorway, all was quiet. Amber was lying on her side, facing away from the door and appeared to be asleep. Gloria walked over to Rebecca and checked her monitoring devices – an automatic self-inflating blood pressure cuff, a pair of electrodes taped to her chest to measure heartbeat and respiration and a small sensor clipped to a finger to measure blood oxygen. An alarm at the control desk would sound if any of these vital signals strayed outside their normal parameters. Gloria was satisfied that Rebecca remained correctly connected. As she looked down, she couldn't help herself, she softly stroked Rebecca's hair and then ran the back of her fingers across Rebecca's cheek.

Amber wasn't asleep. Maybe Gloria knew it, maybe she didn't. Amber didn't care. After talking to Dr. Schade, Amber decided that she and Rebecca were both prisoners of Open Arms and needed to find a way to escape! For several days she watched Rebecca closely, looking for some flicker of awareness. At length she decided that if Rebecca wasn't going to come to her, she'd go to Rebecca. Her first thought was to try poetry. At night after everyone was asleep, she started reciting poems she knew by heart.

DAY 9

"Eye Dropper! Mother, what on earth do you need an eyedropper for?" Elizabeth was both amused and perplexed at the same time.

"None of your business. Just bring me an eyedropper."

Elizabeth looked at her mother and frowned. "Bizarre," that's what she thought. What was happening? Should she alert the staff? "Okay, I'll get you one, but you've got to tell me why."

"If I ask an aide for one, they'll go crazy and think I'm over the edge. I have a few things that I want to do, and I need an eye dropper. Don't be too alarmed. I'm not going to cause any trouble. Please humor me and bring me an eyedropper." Amber glared defiantly at her daughter.

"OK Mom, you win. Why don't we go out to supper tomorrow night and I'll bring it then."

"I can't, we're having pizza tomorrow night."

"Mom, you HATE pizza!"

"It's okay, take me to lunch. Take me to that Chinese buffet. I love their Hot and Sour soup."

"Eye dropper and pizza! Are you sure you're okay?"

"Maybe it's sex! It's been quite a while since I've had any sex. Six years since your dad died. There lots of old geezers here that don't think about anything but sex. Pizza, sex and an eyedropper; what could be more fun."

Elizabeth didn't think Amber was being funny. Her mother seemed to be out of control. This wild outburst could be a sign of Alzheimer's or something like that. She resolved to stop and see Rosemary on the way out. This was serious.

"Elizabeth, trust me, I'm okay. Everything is fine. I need an eyedropper, and the reason is private and I don't want to go out tomorrow because there's something I want to do here and there's no sex here, thank God! If I'm going to live here without going crazy, you'll have to do some things to help me. I need more poetry. Find me another book. All these modern women write about is sex and death. Get me Robert Service and Ogden Nash; I need to laugh at something."

DAY 10

As Gloria reached the doorway she smelled it. Her first thought was that Amber had somehow taken some of the night's pizza back into the room. It wasn't a unique behavior where residents started hoarding food, usually a sign of a more serious mental decline. She turned on her flashlight and scanned the room. Everything seemed in order. Then she looked down and saw the crumpled napkin lying between Amber's and Rebecca's beds, soaked with pizza sauce. Relieved, Gloria picked it up and at the end of her rounds, dropped it in the kitchen trash barrel.

DAY 12

"Can I have a straw?" Amber asked the aide.

The supper was mashed potatoes with hamburger gravy, creamed peas and fruit cup, followed by a desert of butterscotch pudding. Butterscotch pudding was far, very far from being one of Amber's favorite foods. When the aide brought the straw, Amber stuck it into the pudding and sucked as hard as she could. The thick pudding climbed only a short distance into the straw. Satisfied, Amber took the straw; wiped it off, making sure she didn't squeeze out the pudding and slipped the straw into the sleeve of her dress. Supper, she decided, had been a success. She waved to an aide and asked to be taken back to her room explaining that she had a new poetry book to read.

Not being able to walk added a significant barrier to Amber's task. She needed to work undetected and that meant finding a way to get over to Rebecca's bed by herself. If she had time, she found out that she could slide down to the floor, roll onto her stomach, crawling and pulling herself across the room. Getting back was another matter. The first time she tried she couldn't figure out how to pull herself up into her chair. There was a small fuss when the aide found her sitting on the floor next to her chair. Amber lied, saying she was trying to get to the bathroom. She was lectured on using the call cord. They discussed side rails for the bed and even using restraints if they found her on the floor again. Amber had been warned!

"Can you leave me in the wheelchair? I might change my mind later and go play bingo." Amber lied again. She wanted to get to Rebecca's bed and didn't want to risk crawling. There wasn't really enough space in the room for the wheelchair, but the aide didn't mind, she left with Amber still in the wheelchair. The trick now was to keep the chair in the room. Amber could climb out of the wheelchair into her bed or into her regular chair, but as soon as an aide spotted the empty wheelchair, they would take it out of the room and park it in the hallway.

As soon as the aide left, Amber wheeled over to her bed stand and poured a small amount of water from her pitcher into a cup, then she wheeled over to Rebecca's bed.

"Hi Rebecca. Let's have some fun and then I'll read you some poetry." Amber wetted a finger in the water cup and slowly drew the finger across Rebecca's lips. "I don't know if you like butterscotch pudding, but the food here is pretty bland and this is the best I could do." Amber pulled the straw out of her sleeve, slipped it between Rebecca's lips and squeezed a little pudding into Rebecca's mouth. "If you don't want it, just spit it out." Amber reached over and lightly stroked Rebecca's cheek, watching for some reaction. "Maybe I'll get something better for you tomorrow."

I like that voice. Who is it? I wonder, wonder.

"Yesterday my daughter brought me a book of poetry. Here's one you should like." Amber read aloud:

"This is my dream,
It is my own dream,
I dreamt it.
I dreamt that my hair was kempt.
Then I dreamt that my true love unkempt it."

The voice seems far away. I like the voice. Is it talking to me?

Amber reached over and picked up Rebecca's hand and placed it in hers. She turned the hand over and stroked it with her index finger, hoping for some reaction or movement.

Rosemary felt increasing concern for Amber's changed behavior. Switching from abrasive to withdrawn, possibly hoarding food, avoiding interacting with staff and residents alike and spending a lot of time in her room; all signs that to Rosemary indicated that there had been some physiological change effecting Amber. Rosemary arranged a conference with Amber's daughter, Elizabeth, and Amber's primary physician, Dr. Mary Anderson. It was hard to get doctors to come to Open Arms to examine residents, but transporting someone to a doctor's office was tangled with state regulations and Rosemary felt she needed to avoid the chance of violating rules. Dr. Anderson had already arrived and was examining Amber. She would come to Rosemary's office as soon as she was finished. Elizabeth would be arriving any minute.

Dr. Anderson strode into Rosemary's office, grabbed a chair, sat down and looked first at Elizabeth and then at Rosemary and then smiled. "Amber seems fine; in fact, she shows some positive signs of improvement and adjustment. Her physical signs are good too. What concerns do you two have?"

"Well," said Rosemary, "we're concerned about her be becoming increasingly withdrawn and some other unusual behaviors. Your assessment is reassuring, but I'm still concerned that there's something happening with her."

"Mom puzzles me. She's asked me to bring her some bizarre items and won't explain why she wants them. But she does seem more content and occupied. She has even quit complaining about the food.

DAY 17

"Can I have some apple juice today?" Amber smiled at the aide, who turned away to retrieve the requested item. Shortly the aide returned with a small plastic cup of apple juice. Amber smiled. "Thank you," she said. As the aide turned away, Amber slipped the eye dropper out of her sleeve and plunged it into the juice cup, pushed the bulb and filled the dropper. Her table mates were oblivious, and Amber had no trouble concealing the dropper.

The oatmeal and toast disappeared as quickly as the fruit cup did. Amber wanted to get back to Rebecca before her cargo of apple juice leaked out. The aides had become accustomed to leaving her in a wheelchair and letting her return to her room by herself so Amber quickly excused herself, backed up and wheeled away.

"Rebecca, it's me. I have some apple juice for you." Amber took Rebecca's hand and gave it a soft squeeze. She slid the eye dropper between Rebecca's lips. "Today it's apple juice for breakfast." Amber slowly squeezed the bulb.

What do I taste? I like it.

Rebecca licked her lips.

"Oh Sweet Jesus!" Amber held her hand to her mouth as she saw Rebecca's tongue. "You are in there!" Amber could barely contain her glee, clapping her hands and shaking Rebecca's arm.

What's that? Someone has my arm.

DAY 20

Amber's success with the apple juice hadn't been repeated. She was puzzled but undaunted. Maybe, she mused, music was an answer.

"Elizabeth, I'm dying to listen to some opera music. You know what I like. Get me one of those pod things with earphones."

"Mother, you couldn't figure out how to use a cell phone, now you want to try an Ipod and music. I hope you know what you're doing, those things cost a ton, and you have to buy the music."

"Good. I'll be happier with opera to drown out the clatter and constant babble of this place. Take me to lunch and buy me a pod full of opera. Verde operas. All of his operas." Amber beamed in triumph at her success.

"Mother, you are the living end. Where would you like to go for lunch?"

DAY 25

Amber discovered that her little bedside stand would easily and quietly slide. As soon as the hall lights dimmed, she'd drape herself over the stand and push and pull herself across the room to Rebecca's bed. Sitting on the edge of the bed she'd put the little buds from the Ipod into Rebecca's ears. Once she was sure the music was playing, she'd drape herself over the stand and push herself back to her bed. Afraid of falling asleep and leaving Rebecca plugged into the Ipod, she'd set the alarm on her clock radio to go off in an hour.

The radio music woke Amber up as she'd hoped. She shut the alarm off and waited for the night nurse to walk by, that would give her ample time to retrieve the Ipod. The shadow at the door signaled the cursory check by the nurse. Amber slid into action, pushing herself over to Rebecca.

"I hope you liked Aida," Amber whispered as she removed the ear buds.

What sound was that? Can I hear something?

Amber held Rebecca's hand hoping for another signal. Maybe, she thought, she doesn't get turned on by opera, too young for it. As she pushed herself back to bed, she decided to get something more-up-to date like Lady Gaga.

DAY 32

Gloria always arrived to work a few minutes early giving herself time for a half a cup of coffee and a few quiet moments in the dining room, settling herself for the day ahead. She truly enjoyed her work, but dealing with so many people struggling with physical and mental issues caused her great stress. She needed those quiet moments with the hot coffee to steel her for the day ahead; ending her reverie with the same short prayer, "Oh God, bring joy and comfort."

Today Gloria strode out of the dining room toward her first task, helping the residents get up and get to breakfast. Speed and efficiency were the hallmarks of the morning effort. Everyone needs some kind of help, getting out of bed, toilet, dressing, wheelchairs and walkers. Working her way down the hall, Gloria arrived at Amber and Rebecca's room. Amber was awake but silent, looking at Gloria with half-closed eyes. Gloria pulled the bedcovers back and helped Amber sit up and swing her legs over the edge of the bed.

"Let me take a quick look at Rebecca." Gloria let go of Amber and stepped over to Rebecca's bed. Lying face down on Rebecca's stomach was a small picture frame. Gloria picked it up and turned it over and saw a young girl in a white dress standing under a trellis.

"Amber, is this your picture?" Gloria took the picture over to Amber.

"Yes. Where'd you get it? Have you been going through my things?"

"Somehow it got on Rebecca's bed. Did you put it there?"

Amber was silent and Gloria just laid the picture on Amber's dresser. "Come on, we've got to get you ready for breakfast."

Gloria decided not to report the discovery. She'd already figured out that Amber had taken an interest in Rebecca but didn't want anyone prying or questioning. Amber was occupied and easier to deal with and what she was doing with Rebecca wasn't much more than reading to her and talking to her so it would be their secret.

DAY 40

The sound of running water puzzled Rebecca. Where was she? The sound was a stream or brook, washing over rocks and gurgling onward. Rebecca smiled, of course it was Pleasure Creek, and she was standing in the water. She wiggled her toes and felt the sand and pebbles and cool water. She didn't move; she just stood there wiggling her toes.

Amber was asleep so she never saw Rebecca smile and couldn't see Rebecca's toes wiggle. Doctor Schade never answered Amber's question about comatose dreams. Amber tried everything to get some response from Rebecca; food, music, poetry; but Rebecca remains asleep. Each day the physical therapy staff hauls Rebeca away and stretches her, messages her, bathes her and then returns her to a freshly made bed but Rebecca is unchanged. Amber has not given up; if anything, she's more determined than ever.

"What can I do to wake you up?" Amber asked. "Where is the key to your brain?"

Amber thought of telling Elizabeth about her efforts to arouse Rebecca but worried that Elizabeth wouldn't understand. She guessed that Gloria knew what she was doing and was glad that Gloria chose not to interfere.

DAY 50

The change is so gradual no one notices. Amber sleeps a little later, talks a little less, doesn't eat quite as much and yet still seems active. Just yesterday at the afternoon social hour she read aloud the Robert Lewis Service poem "The Cremation of Sam McGee." Gloria seemed to sense the change in Amber before anyone else did. Ever since the arrival of Rebecca, everyone noticed that Amber's mood was lighter, and her temper flared far less often. Now Gloria began to sense something else was happening to Amber. Even Amber sensed that she was changing.

Amber was half dozing when Sharon arrived. "Hello Amber, I hope I didn't wake you."

"No, you didn't and it's nice to see you again. Rebecca and I always love company." Amber smiled. Sharon smiled back and sat down on Rebecca's bed.

"Hello darling. You look good today; someone has fixed your hair."

"I have something to tell you." Amber spoke with a hesitant pause. "I hope you won't be angry, but I've been trying to help Rebecca wake up." Having let the cat out of the bag, there was no going back, and Amber explained everything she'd done over the past two months, food, music, poetry and conversation. "Sometimes I'm sure she knows I'm here. She licked her lips once and also puckered when I put a few drops of grapefruit juice in her mouth. I think she hears the music but doesn't seem to like opera I guess."

Sharon was startled at first and then was annoyed, but for just an instant. She took a deep breath and started to cry and then burst out laughing. "Amber, you're an angel! We've all been helpless but not you! Please tell me more, I'm so excited, she licked her lips. "Oh goodness gracious!"

DAY 51

Amber's revelation resulted in general turmoil in the staff of Open Arms. At last, it was decided that the only prudent way to handle Amber's independent physio-therapy was to ignore it. Sharon Russel called Dr. Schade and asked him to visit Amber and he said he'd do that as quickly as he could, and he arrived late in the afternoon.

"I've heard you've become an angel," Dr. Schade said as he walked into Amber's room.

Amber smiled. "Do people in a coma dream? I asked you that once and you never gave me an answer."

"What do you think?"

"I'm sure they do and I'm sure that Rebecca does too."

"What do we do now? I don't see much change in Rebecca, but I think your efforts are more than worthwhile. Will you continue your therapy?"

"My doctor says I'm weakening, and she doesn't know why. I want so much to see Rebecca awake."

"Rosemary tells me that they will make some changes that will make it easier for you to work with Rebecca."

DAY 52

Gloria wheeled Amber back to her room after dinner. The room had been re-arranged to make spce for a wheelchair so Amber could get over to Rebecca's bed. Gloria had reminded Amber that no one should know about her giving Rebecca stuff she smuggled out of the dining room. It was mid-October, so darkness came early. Amber turned on her reading light and reached over to her bedside table and picked up her favorite book of poetry. She thumbed through the pages and stopped at one of her favorites. Looking out the window over Rebecca's bed she could see the almost full moon rise. She knew the verses by heart, so she turned out the light leaving the room bathed in the quiet dim moonlight.

"Rebecca, this is one of my favorites and I know it by heart, so I'll read it in the moonlight."

Moonlight on the garden,
Music moves our souls,
Your body touches mine,
We dance together under a trellis,
We are single rhythmic movement,
Dancing on the moonlight.

Hear the music in the darkness,
Warm, the breeze caresses,
Soft, my skirt swirls,
Your breath in my hair,
Your touch on my neck,
We are single rhythmic movement,
Dancing on the moonlight.

The world whispers to us,
We hear the murmur of singing voices,
Their song caresses our hearts,
Their words are our music of love,
We are single rhythmic movement,
Dancing on the moonlight.

"I see the moonlight!"
Amber heard the soft voice and smiled. The book of poems slipped from her hands and fell to the floor with a loud thump. Amber could no longer hear it.

Rebecca heard it.

Walking Home

George opened one eye and cautiously surveyed the room. Satisfied he was alone, he pushed the covers back and sat up slowly, swinging his feet over the edge of the bed. The early morning light reflecting off the concrete patio outside his window brightened up the room. A slight smile played across his face as George stood up, holding onto the bed to keep his balance. After steadying himself he walked stiffly into the bathroom, closed the door behind him and tried to lock it. He fumbled for a bit and gave up.

"It looks like a nice day," George muttered to himself as he turned on the water in the sink. George talked when he was alone. It didn't sound like he was talking to himself and if you overheard him; you'd expect someone to answer. Often George paused as though he too was expecting an answer.

Opening the medicine cabinet, he took out a comb, turned a faucet and swished the comb through the stream water and combed the thin silver hair back across his head.

"Hardly worth it anymore," he said aloud without looking at the mirror.

He washed his face slowly, soaping his hands and rubbing them around his cheeks and over his forehead and sticking his soapy fingers in his ears. Rinsing the soap from his hands, he splashed the warm water over his face until he felt all the soap was gone. Then he groped for a towel and dried his eyes and chest. Still dripping water from his chin, he took a can of shaving cream off the shelf over the toilet and squirted a large mound onto his left hand and then spread the creamy lather over his face. He shaved with short, slow strokes as though the whiskers were being pulled out painfully one at a time. Between each stroke he rinsed the razor clean. After the last razor stroke, he repeated the rinsing ritual, splashing water over his face until the remaining streaks of lather were gone. Rubbing his face briskly with the towel he smiled in self-satisfaction; shaving always made him feel ready for the day.

"Chores are done." He tried to unlock the door without success, turned the handle and opened it.

Norma had just gotten herself a fresh cup of coffee and was on her way back to the nursing desk when she heard the water running as she passed George's room. She opened the door just as he stepped out of the bathroom. He stopped and looked down. George wore only undershorts to bed; they'd tried, without success, to get him to wear pajamas or at least a nightshirt. "Strangles my arms, can't sleep," was his reply. Now he looked down, embarrassed at the baggy grey undershorts.

"You're up early this morning."

"I'm done with chores. Who are you?"

"George, I'm Norma. You know that." Norma smiled and held out her hand to help him back to the bed.

He drew away.

"I don't know you at all. I know my brother Ed and I know my wife Hazel and I know my son Roger and my daughter Florence, but I sure don't know you. Why are you here?"

"George, I've worked here for almost twenty years, and you've lived here for five years."

"I don't live here. I live west of Fulda."

Norma smiled, turned around and walked back out into the corridor. She liked George, he was never friendly, but he was never crabby or mean either. He took good care of himself and got along with everyone. At ninety-four it was amazing how much he could do; he just couldn't seem to remember where he was and what he was doing here. She looked at the clock.

"Seven thirty and he's already done with chores. I wonder what time he got up on the farm." Norma left George and walked toward her station.

George put on his favorite shirt, a long sleeved light blue denim work shirt. Then he took two pairs of white socks out of the top dresser drawer and walked over by the window to a small wooden chair and sat down. He had a hard time putting on socks and two pairs were going to be almost impossible. He couldn't bend over far enough to use both hands, so it was a slow process. First, he held the sock with one hand and slipped his toes in, then he pushed his foot along the floor to slide the sock on as far as it would go and then he could pull it over the heel with one hand. Getting a second sock over the first required repeated pushing and pulling and tugging before his foot felt comfortable.

When the last sock was on, he sat still for a while and looked out the window. The trees along the backyard were just starting to show a tinge of color and the sumac bushes across the fence were almost red. It had been a cool summer, and signs of fall were showing up early.

"Better get going before it freezes. The corn ain't dented and the beans got a ways to go."

He pushed himself up from the chair and pulled open the bottom drawer of the dresser, lifted out a pair of almost new bib overalls and put them on. Fishing a well-worn pair of high-topped work shoes from under the bed he slid his feet into them. With two pairs of socks the shoes felt nice and snug. Walking back to the window he sat down and bent to the task of tying. Working with the socks had loosened him up enough so that he could bend over just far enough to tie each shoe. He double knotted each bow to make sure they wouldn't come untied.

"I'm glad that's done."

The door swung inward, and Norma stuck her head in.

"Breakfast is ready. Let's go eat." Norma held the door open and smiled at George.

"We always have breakfast right after chores. Is Hazel in the kitchen?"

Norma took George's arm and led him down the hall toward the dining room.

"You've got your work clothes on today, getting ready to pick corn?"

"No. Corn's not ready. Where's Hazel?"

Norma led George to a table. Herman, from across the hall, was already there in his wheelchair. Herman was only sixty-eight, slight and stooped, one side of his face smiling and the other expressionless.

"Gu oaring Sheorge." Herman raised his right hand in greeting and tilted his head sideways to look up at George and Norma.

"Do you know my brother Ed?" George sat down next to Herman. Norma patted George on the shoulder and walked away.

"We buy our cattle at the Livestock Pavilion in Slayton. Ed sure knows how to spot good stock cows. Do you live in Slayton?"

Herman shook his head no.

A dining room worker wheeled a breakfast cart up to the table and slid a glass of orange juice, a cup of coffee and a bowl of oatmeal to both George and Herman.

"Would you like some toast," the server asked?

Herman nodded and the cook handed them each a plate of toast.

"I'm going home today." George put two spoons full of sugar in his coffee.

"Is su one couing to get ou?" Herman asked in a wistfully soft voice.

"We've got some cattle to load up and it's time get the corn picker ready. It don't pay to hurry with a corn picker. All you get is breakdowns and lost time looking for parts."

"I wish I cou go hoe." Herman stirred his oatmeal without looking at George. "There's no un to cou and get me."

The two finished their meal in silence. By the time they were done the dining room was full and noisy. George slid his chair back and slowly pushed himself up.

"If you see Hazel, tell her I'm on my way."

Herman turned his head sideways and looked up at George.

"Ha a nice tri."

George stopped when he got to the hallway. He stood there until Norma saw him and walked over.

"I don't know if you're lost or you just want a pretty girl to walk you back to your room." Norma put her arm around him. George started walking as if on cue.

Alone in his room again, George went back to the dresser, pulled out the top drawer, felt around under a pile of handkerchiefs, pulled out a silver pocket watch and held it up by a braided leather cord. He wound it slowly, shook it and then held it up to his ear. Nodding with satisfaction at the soft, steady clicking, he dropped the watch into a breast pocket of the overalls and looped the end of the cord over a button. Turning back to the dresser, he reached into the drawer again and brought out pair of grey socks.

Sticking his into the bundle, he extracted a small pocketknife with ivory handles.

"This is a good knife. I never lost it either. Ed told me when he gave it to me to be careful and never lose it. I was ten years old." He let the knife lay in the palm of his left hand and slowly stroked the yellowed ivory with his thumb.

The knife was a powerful talisman to him. When his son, Roger, brought him here, George had taken the knife out of his pocket and slipped it in his shoe. The admitting nurse had asked if George had anything sharp like a straight-edged razor or a pocketknife. Roger said he didn't think so. A nurse went through everything anyway, but they never found the knife. George always kept it hidden in a pair of socks, though he often carried it in his pocket, being able to touch the knife made him feel connected.

He opened the small blade and touched it lightly with his thumb. "Better put an edge on it when I get home." He closed the blade and slipped the knife into his right pants pocket. He took an old worn coin purse and billfold off the dresser top. The coin purse went in his left pants pocket and the billfold in his right back pocket.

George turned toward the door to his room and without looking back, strode purposely out into the hall and toward the main lobby.

Norma should have seen George leave; he walked right past her and out the front door. She had stopped to see if Herman needed any help turning on the TV. George walked right by as she put her head in Herman's door.

The receptionist at the front desk should have seen George leave, but she was taking a phone message and dropped her pencil. George walked right by the desk as she bent down to pick up the pencil.

Ron Chambers, the business manager, should have seen George go by his office window as he walked through the front doors. He had just started reading the new state reporting forms for patient evaluations and distressed by what he read he put his hands over his eyes.

George stood outside the front door for a few seconds and then started walking. He automatically turned west, towards Fulda.

George and Ed farmed together for over fifty years on the home place where they'd been born and grew up. When George married Hazel, Ed moved into town. Hazel wanted a new house but somehow it never came to be, and she had to be content with the old square farmhouse, with the long porch facing the road, the drafty windows and the cold floors. Hazel slowly stopped complaining about the house, she came to understand that it was as much a part of George as she had become.

At first his steps were slow and halting, but he was rejuvenated as he walked, he straightened up, took longer strides and started to swing his arms. What breeze there was, was warm and full of the scents of fall.

Whenever he met a car, George raised his hand and held up one finger as a fraternal greeting, just as he always did whenever he met a neighbor on the road. He fit so naturally into the serenity of the autumn countryside that no one even noticed him ambling slowly along the roadside.

"Forgot my cap. Better stop at the Co-op and see if they have any giveaways." George said to himself as he headed west. He stayed on the sidewalk until he got to the edge of town.

Ed was four years older than George. When Ed died at eighty, Roger tried to talk his dad into retiring and moving to town.

"Go to town and die of boredom, not me, not on your life. This is where I belong. Ain't that right, Hazel?"

Hazel would smile and nod. She did convince George to rent out half the farm. "Give some young fellow a chance to see what he can do. Don't keep hogging all the land for yourself."

They did go to Phoenix after Christmas one year, the only real trip they ever took. "Hazel got tired of muddy boots all winter. I told her we'll sell the cattle and take the money somewhere warm this year." Without Ed's acumen for livestock, George found it hard to keep a cattle herd going anyway.

"I didn't like Phoenix one bit," George exclaimed when they got back. "There are so many old coots standing around down there with their hands in their pockets you can't find enough bare ground to spit on."

Hazel died and still George stayed on, renting out the rest of the land and living alone in the house. He did start going to town almost every day, playing a few hands of pinochle with friends at the Silver Dollar Cafe.

Roger made it a point to stop at the cafe two or three times a week for coffee, that way he could check up on George without causing any fuss. On Sundays he and his wife Margaret would drive out to the farm, pick up George and take him into Fulda for Mass at St. Gabriel's. After Mass they would fix dinner at the farm, do the dishes and a little house cleaning. When Hazel died, Margaret started doing George's laundry. She came out on Wednesdays, while George was in town.

Susan Johnson was tired after working all night, but she didn't care, it was such a perfect day that she wanted to take her time getting home. When she saw the old man walking, she slowed and put down the window.

"Hi there. Need a lift?"

"Oh, no thanks. I'm just walking home. Feels good to be outdoors." George smiled and leaned over to see who it was.

"Well, be careful of the traffic." Susan rolled up the window and drove off. Looking in the rear-view mirror she saw him giving a friendly wave.

When George's driver's license expired, he had to retake the test and failed. The next Sunday, Roger spent all afternoon convincing George to move into town.

"Dad, you can't see good enough to drive."

"I'll drive slower."

"They'll take away your car."

"I'll drive the tractor."

"You don't have a tractor anymore."

"I was just kidding. I'll have Lester Jenasko take me to town."

"Lester doesn't drive anymore; he's as blind as you are."

"Who'll look after the house?"

George never said he'd move, he just stopped arguing. Roger packed some clothes and things, and they left. George never looked back as the car started down the driveway; he sat staring straight ahead with his arms folded defiantly.

Both of Roger's girls were in college and the spare bedroom suited George nicely so his move to town went smoothly. Every morning about nine o'clock, he'd walk up to the Silver Dollar and enjoy an hour with his "Geezers" as he called them. The three-block walk limbered him up a bit and the exercise kept him more alert.

It started a few days after Christmas. The girls had left to go back to college and the winter wind was so strong that Margaret asked George if he'd like her to drive him to the Silver Dollar.

George looked at Margaret for a moment and then said, "You're not Hazel."

Margaret looked at George. "Are you all right," she asked?

"I thought for a minute that you were Hazel."

It wasn't ever very obvious at first, but George's world began to slowly drift in time. He began to talk about farming as though he still had field work to do. He began to talk about Hazel as though she was still alive. One morning he left home for the Silver Dollar and about an hour later a Sheriff's Deputy brought him back saying he'd been walking along Highway 59 and someone recognized him and called 911.

"Well, I can't drive, and I need to get to the Farm. Ed'll need help getting ready to plant. Seems like I'm letting him do all the work."

Margaret and Roger started keeping a closer eye on George. He still walked to the café, but Margaret stood by the door and watched to make sure he headed in the right direction and then called Roger to let him know that George was on his way. That worked for a while, but soon they had to spend way too much of their time watching George.

"Dad, there's something we need to talk about," was how Roger started the conversation. He explained how isolated George was in their home, how hard it was becoming for him to walk to the Silver Dollar, how much work it was to keep him safe and comfortable. "Dad, it's time we looked at what's best for you."

They took George to the Clinic in Worthington. The outcome wasn't a surprise, Dementia. The solution wasn't a surprise either; supervised living arrangements and therapy are the best solution. George was heading for a facility that offered what was euphemistically described as a "Memory Unit."

Golden Days Care Center in Windom had an opening. Roger, Margaret and George visited them on Sunday and George moved in the following Thursday.

There was no fuss and George never complained. He was beginning to become slowly detached from life around him and spending more time wandering in his past.

George was missed just after breakfast. The police and the sheriff were notified, and a neighborhood search was started. Wandering away doesn't happen often and when it happens during warm weather there isn't as much panic as there is in the winter; still, there's a serious effort to find the missing resident quickly. One policeman headed for the Des Moines River to look along the banks; with low water level it didn't seem likely George had been swept away, but he might just be sitting there watching the river. A patrol car drove up and down the city streets asking pedestrians if they'd seen a slow-moving elderly gentleman in bib overalls. At eleven o'clock they started knocking on doors and the Sheriff's department started a systematic patrol pattern on all the roads leading out of town.

George stood and watched Susan drive away. He gave her a wave as he watched. Resuming his walk, he saw the farmhouse sitting back from the road. George smiled and turned up the grassy driveway into an old school yard where a weathered but sturdy one-room schoolhouse stood, vacant and quiet. It had been quite a long time since children had run and played in the broad school yard. "TALCOT LAKE TOWN HALL" emblazoned over the door signaled its new purpose. A hand pump waited nearby, and a pair of swings still hung from the rusty steel tube frame. George smiled as he stepped to the pump and began to work the handle, looking in vain for the cup he kept hanging there by a wire.

George was pleased to see the house looking so nice. His mind had easily transformed the old country school into his beloved farm home.

"Hazel, I know you don't like me to drink from the yard well but why do you hide my cup!"

Water flowed easily and George cupped his free hand to catch a cool drink. Wiping his hands on his overalls, he walked over to the porch, climbed the steps and walked to the front door. He smiled when he saw the picture of a deer leaping over a brook etched into the oval frosted glass pane. He reached out and tapped the glass lightly. Reassured, he reached down and grasped the doorknob; a heavy, cast brass oval-shaped knob covered with a fine geometric pattern. George twisted and pulled to open the door. He frowned when the knob came off in his hand.

"I've fiddled with that knob, but it always comes loose. I guess I'll have to find a screwdriver and fix it again."

He dropped the knob in his pocket, walked over to the steps and sat down, glad to be back home.

Margaret answered the phone and listened intently as the Business Manager, Ron Chambers, explained that George apparently had gotten outside and wandered away. "We monitor the front door very closely, but it happens sometimes. I wouldn't worry because we haven't lost anyone yet." Ron paused. "We'll have him back pretty quickly."

Sheriff's Deputy Sandy Woodkey was headed west along highway 82, scanning from side-to-side looking for George. As he drove by the old Talcott Lake school house, he glanced up the driveway and saw someone sitting on the steps by the front door. He called dispatch to let them know he thought he'd spotted George. Sandy swung the patrol car around, turned into the schoolyard, slowly rolled up to the school and stopped just short of the steps. George was leaning back against the door with his hands in his pockets. "Dispatch, unit seven, it looks like this guy needs some help, can you send an ambulance. I'm leaving the squad to have a look."

Sandy got out of the squad car and walked over to George.

"Hi old timer," He called out.

George was leaning back against the school door with his eyes closed and a slight smile on his face. He didn't respond to Sandy's greeting; he was too far away; he'd finished walking home.

***

Roger and Margaret sat in Mr. Chambers' office, waiting impatiently for Chambers to arrive. At last, he strode into the office, said hello, shook their hands perfunctorily, expressed remorse and sorrow at George's demise and sat down. They waited expectantly. Mr. Chambers set a small cardboard box on the table in front of them and explained that it contained what they found in George's pockets; a small penknife "maybe you recognize it looks like he's had it for a long time," a handkerchief, a short pencil, a coin purse, a billfold and a pocket watch "must've been a treasured possession." He lifted the watch out of the box and laid it on the table. Without comment Mr. Chambers reached into the box and took out a cast brass doorknob, oval-shaped, decorated with a fine geometric pattern. Roger looked at the knob, looked at Margaret then looked at Mr. Chambers and shook his head.

"How on earth did that knob get in his pocket? That's the doorknob from our front door at the farm!"

One Sunday Morning

The Monsoon season is passing, and Thailand is switching from rainy to hot. The wet jungles drive up the humidity and short bursts of rain are quickly forming clouds that weave in and out of the sky. The Vietnam War is grinding on and the effort to stop the flow of Viet Cong supplies coming down the Ho Chi Minh Trail means stepped up US Air Force raids. Air Bases in Udorn and Ubon are putting forth maximum efforts, pounding the jungle trails.

The rain stopped at dawn, but puddles still dot Ubon's concrete ramps and taxiways. The horizon is shrouded in haze and the morning heat clings damply, dimming the sun behind a steamy mist roiling up from the rice paddies and jungle that surround the airfield. Pairs of men, dressed in flight suits and survival vests, carrying kneeboards and helmets, walk slowly along the ramp heading for a row of dull green F4D Phantom jets. The planes have their canopies open, ground crews busily preparing them for the approaching fliers, starting units idle with their umbilicals mated into each plane's belly, wheeled red fire extinguishers stand ominously close, rockets and bombs hang pendulously under the wings with their yellow and red arming streamers twisting fitfully in the humid air.

Stan and Norm stop at the first plane in line. The crew chief stands on a ladder leading to the cockpit, ready for the pre-flight inspection. Stan tosses the crew chief his helmet and begins his walk-around inspection. He starts at the left wing, checking each rocket and bomb, running his hands along the slats and flaps, pushing on inspection plates and dabbing his fingers on joints looking for loose bolts and tell-tale hydraulic oil leaks. It's a routine done with methodical precision, no item is missed, no trouble in the air because of something overlooked on the ground.

By the time Stan worked his way around the plane, Norm is already buckled in the back seat of the cramped cockpit and is head down, busily engaged in his own pre-flight check list.

"Short and hot," Stan says to the crew chief as he stands by the ladder into the cockpit.

The crew chief frowns. Short and hot means close-in attacks on enemy targets, heavy ground fire and a high risk of being hit.

"You don't need to bring me back any bullet holes Colonel."

"All I want to bring you back is my sweet ass." Stan grins up at the crew chief.

The crew chief slides down the ladder and Stan quickly climbs up and drops into the front cockpit, bends down and buckles his seat belt and shoulder harness. He takes off his dark blue flight cap and pulls a blue silk skullcap out of his helmet. He tugs the skullcap down over his close-cropped, curly blond hair, slowly slides on the helmet and then plugs in the radio and oxygen lines.

"Intercom check."

"Intercom check," Norm answers, his voice has an electronic twang in Stan's helmet.

With mechanical precision the two men step through the pre-flight check-list routine, no item is missed, no chance for trouble in the air because something was ignored on the ground, use every extra margin of safety. At last Stan raises his hand to the crew chief who quickly sprints to the front of the plane.

Down the row of planes other crew chiefs are lining up in front of their planes. Stan twirls a gloved finger and the starting unit barks. Soon the whine of jet turbines drowns out all other sounds, sooty heat waves billow over the concrete and the remaining puddles disappear in a cloud of kerosene scented spray. Stan's plane slowly rolls forward, the whine deepening into a throaty roar. As the canopy descends the roar diminishes into a soft whistle inside the cockpit.

"Ubon Ground Control, Delta-one. Delta Flight ready to taxi. Request clearance to the active runway."

"Delta-one, barometer two-niner-eight-two. Winds two-four-zero six knots. Visibility three miles. Proceed to two-seven left and hold short in the arming safety zone".

"Delta-one two-seven left," Stan repeats as he adjusts the altimeter to the barometric pressure.

"Delta-two." Stan's Wingman acknowledges the ground controller's instructions.

"Delta -three."

"Delta-four."

The four planes making up Delta Flight roll slowly along in single file toward the runway. Cockpits full of radios, radars, computers and weapon guidance systems quickly heat up the cockpit and in the tropical sun; it becomes furnace hot by the end of the short trip. Stan pulls a large red bandanna out of a leg pouch in his flight suit and wipes his dripping face. Behind him Norm is doing the same thing.

The planes pause just short of runway two-seven. From a small hut, four airmen run out - one to each of the Delta Flight planes and quickly pull the safety pins out of the bombs and rockets and then run back to the hut, the red and yellow arming ribbons trailing behind them.

"Delta Flight, contact tower on one-two-one point seven."

"Delta Flight going to one-two-one point seven." Stan resets the radio receiver to the new frequency. "Ubon Tower, Delta flight ready for departure."

"Delta-Two ready."

"Delta-Three ready."

"Delta-Four ready."

"Delta Flight, Ubon tower, you are cleared for takeoff. Good hunting."

"Delta-one." Stan pushes the throttles forward and the whistle loudens to a screech and then explodes with a roar as he ignites the afterburners. As the plane gathers speed Stan checks and is reassured that his wingman is right alongside. At eighty knots Stan pulls back slightly on the control stick raising the plane's nose and lifting the nose wheel off the runway. Norm calls out the airspeed so Stan can concentrate on the runway. "Ninety. One-ten. One-thirty." At One hundred and fifty knots there's a slight thump as the main landing gear lifts off the runway. Stan holds the nose down to let the speed increase before climbing. No chances, nothing forgotten on the ground that could cause trouble in the air, use every extra margin of safety. At last Stan pulls back on the control stick to raise the nose further and the jet soars above the runway trailing tentacles of white mist in its wake. The wingman's plane is close on the right wingtip. Stan cuts off the afterburner and adjusts to best rate of climb.

"Delta Flight, turn right to three-six-zero. Climb to two-two thousand." Norm's voice sounds far away over the intercom. They're only four feet apart, but the only possible physical contact would be for Norm to tap Stan on the shoulder. Stan can't even turn around far enough to see Norm in the claustrophobic cockpit.

The cloud tops are brilliant in the clear cool air above the Thailand jungle. The rice paddies and jungle below are blurred by a smoky blue haze that makes the green jungle foliage look almost black. The four plane Delta flight forms into a spread formation - Delta-one in the lead, Delta-two to the right and slightly below, Delta-three behind and slightly above Delta-one and Delta-four behind and above Delta-three. The flight vanishes into the cloud dappled sky leaving only a faint rumble and a few greasy smudges against the clouds.

The intercom is silent as the two men concentrate on their tasks. The silence isn't boredom or nonchalance or indifference; it's passage from the known into the unknown, from safety into danger.

There's nothing left to say when the airfield sinks behind the misty black hills and you're alone and naked, far above the earth; not even the massive machine gives you any comfort. Norm navigates to the target and Stan keeps them flying. If you're busy you don't think about what's coming or at least you don't think too much about it.

Their destination and target is between a pair of low jungle-covered hills set beside a muddy stream in Laos. The morning briefing described the importance of clearing those hills to prevent attacks on a fire base just downstream in Vietnam.

"Target coming up," Norm's voice breaks the silence. "Is it in the clear?"

"I've got the stream. The hills are a little cloudy. Looks good to me. Let's get this done and go home. Delta Flight, Switch to FAC frequency."

Stan switches to his second radio transmitter to the frequency used by the Forward Air Controller who will direct them to their target approach.

"Ginger-five, Delta Flight overhead and we have a visual target."

The Forward Air Controller pulls back on the throttles of his OV-10 observation plane and turns toward the two hills. He'll glide down to about five hundred feet above the jungle and then fire two white phosphorus smoke rockets to mark the target.

"Hi Delta Flight. We've got friendlies fifteen miles east if you have to go over the side. Fly New York to Chicago with HEF to open things up a bit and then we'll give them nape and fry some rice. I'll fire two Willie Peters so aim between them." The little silver plane bounces downward toward the stream and the dark hills with the engines idling so he can get closer before the hidden enemy hears him and start shooting.

Stan sets the weapons selection switches on the "dog bone" to release four five-hundred-pound high explosive fragmentation bombs. The first pass will be with high explosives and the second will be napalm and rockets. New York to Chicago directs them to attack from east to west; they'll come out of the sun, across the stream, up and over the hills - thirty seconds apart.

"Ginger-five. Delta Flight with HEF from New York."
"Delta-Two."
"Delta-Three."
"Delta-Four."
Ginger-five watches as the two white phosphorus rockets whistle toward their targets and explode into balls of white smoke. Satisfied, he pushes the throttles all the way forward. With a roar, the small plane banks sharply downward and back toward the stream. The plane builds up speed at tree-top level, crossing the

stream Ginger-five pulls back on the stick and the little plane leaps back into the sky.

"Ginger-five, we have your smoke and have you clear of the target. Delta Flight, tallyho!"

"Delta-Two."

"Delta-Three."

"Delta-Four."

The four planes turn east, away from the target and form into single file behind Stan in the lead plane. As soon as they're lined up the first plane banks sharply to the left and down into a steep rolling dive. Stan groans as the G-force of the steep bank squeezes him into the seat. Resting his thumb on the "pickle button", he lines up the plane's nose between the two pillows of smoke and watches the gun sight as the "piper" slides toward to his aiming point. Throttles back, speed brake doors open, slats and flaps deployed, the F4D is no longer flying toward the target, it's falling toward the target. Small, bright orange dots appear to float above the jungle, winking and dancing with angry, feverish energy. Stan squeezes his thumb down and the plane jerks as the bombs fall free. Throttles full forward, close speed brake doors, light afterburners. The plane rolls to the right, climbing quickly away from the hills and the deadly dancing orange dots of enemy anti-aircraft fire. Stan feels something hit his left leg as the plane rises over the hills. A bright-red fire warning light starts blinking furiously. He pulls the fire-suppression lever and then automatically arms the canopy ejection system.

"Delta-one breaking off. I think we caught one. You okay Norm?"

"Nothing back here. Everything looks green."

With heart-stopping suddenness the instrument panel now blazes with red and yellow lights: hydraulic pressure, fuel pressure, engine temperature, electrical power.

"Hang on Norm, I'm heading for the pick-up zone, we're getting outta here. Ginger-five, Delta-one over the side. Delta-two, you've got the flight."

The plane vibrates and slews drunkenly eastward trailing thick black smoke. Stan jerks the canopy release and then pulls the rear-seat ejection handle. With a soft thump, he feels Norm's ejection seat fire. Now it's his turn, Stan's head slams into his chest and a sharp pain shoots up his back as his own seat explodes from the dying plane.

Two parachutes glide slowly and quietly downward toward the black jungle; sounds of combat fade quickly in the misty hills. Dazed for a moment, Stan loses track of the ground, seeing only dark shadows in all directions. Reaching up to rub his eyes he discovers his helmet has slid down over his face and the shadows are only a reflection of light from the faceplate. With the helmet back in place he looks down at a brushy clearing pockmarked by muddy bomb craters. Stan landed hard enough to black out.

With the early morning sun at his back, Stan drove dreamily along the vacant highway. He smiled at the silver water tower peeped over the trees. The trip from Omaha to Mankato took him just over three hours. His timing was almost perfect, just before noon; He knew he'd catch his dad at the Inn.

Mankato, Kansas, sits astride US Highway 36, just south of the Nebraska border; wheat country with low undulating hills, cottonwoods and willows huddling in the creek bottoms leaving the hilltops bare to the sky. The gentle but steady western wind creates surf-like waves as it slides across the fields of ripening wheat. Bobolinks and meadowlarks call from their fence post lookouts to no one in particular. The skyline is broken only by an occasional windmill or steeple or far off water tower. In the fall the air will be hazy and dusty and dry and smoke-blue, but today it's clear and soft and smells of grass and clover. Elms and Maples shade Mankato's sturdy square prairie houses and neat white bungalows with their heavy posted porches. Zinnias and pansies and nasturtiums and hollyhocks splash color on the green lawns. Sunday morning, slow, soft, lazy and quiet.

Stan at a man walking slowly across his yard, one hesitant step at a time. Like a great blue heron, eyes downward, he searches the grass, stops, and then plunges the dandelion fork with death dealing swiftness and pries out an offending plant.

"Harold!" His wife's voice booms through the open screen door. "Come on in and get ready. I told mother we'd meet them in Lovewell and drive out to the reservoir together."

Harold surveys the lawn as though he expects it to be covered with dandelions by the time he gets back and then begins to walk slowly toward the front steps.

Pass ing nearby house, Stan inhales the smells of frying chicken and fresh-sliced tomatoes and sweet corn that waft tantalizingly from an open window. Silverware clatters and dishes rattle against an oak table.

"Don't forget the extra saltshaker" comes a mother's voice from the direction of the kitchen.

"Jimmy, don't do that! Mom, Jimmy threw salt at me."

"Sissy! Can't take it, can't take it."

"Jimmy! You finish setting the table. Donna, you come out here and help me. Sometimes you want to tear your hair out."

On a shady porch, Stan sees a man wearing a frayed undershirt, and paint-stained pants sitting in a large fan backed wicker chair, bare feet up on a small ottoman, reading the Sunday paper. As he turns each page, he stops to take a sip from a tall glass of lemonade, making a soft smacking sound with his lips when he puts the glass down.

Downtown, the front doors of the Methodist Church stand wide open, even though the congregation has vanished. The thumping sound of hymn books being piled in stacks at the pew ends gives the lone usher away. Across the street the shady square is empty and serene, dappled with sunlight.

Last night downtown Mankato was busy, boisterous and crowded. Cars and pickups sat shoulder to shoulder at the curb, men stood with one foot up on the bumper or the running board, their cigarettes glowing in the twilight, talking about crops and prices and baseball and weather. Women strolled along the sidewalks, stopping to window shop and greet neighbors and friends. Boys ran through the shadows of the square, yelling wildly, waving their arms with abandon. Girls stood in self-conscious groups under the streetlights, hoping someone in particular would notice them. Now the square is neatly empty, the storefronts seem new and fresh; the streets swept clean by the late Sunday morning sunlight. Downtown looks dressed up for Sunday.

Stan sees an old black car idling slowly down the far end of Main Street. As it turns east around the corner, a neatly painted sign, "BOB'S INN", is visible on the car door. The car pulls over in front of a small white wooden building on the south side of the street. In the windows, darkened neon beer signs wait quietly and a worn "CLOSED" sign hangs limply on the door. Bob Standerwick climbs slowly out of the car and walks to the door, selecting the proper key, inserting it in the lock, turning it, pushing the door open and flipping the light switch with a continuous motion honed by twenty years of repetition.

Bob is tall and lean with thinning sandy hair. He has a long narrow face with deeply creased cheeks and long ears. His expression would look forlorn if it wasn't for the mischievous twinkle that lights his blue eyes. On Sunday, Bob always comes down to the Inn to "check the coolers." Walking behind the short counter, he slides open the cover of each cooler and squeezes a beer bottle. Satisfied that everything is running properly, he turns to the small backroom and checks the back door making sure it's still locked.

Stan pulls in beside the old black car and steps out. He limps as he walks to the Inn's door.

"Hey Dad."

The sound of his son's voice startled Bob enough to make him jump.

"Well for gosh sake where'd you come from? I didn't even hear you pull up. When did you get back?" Bob turned around, walked over to his son and slapped him on the back.

Stan took off his sunglasses and sat down on a stool at the end of the counter. "I flew into Offet last night. Ever since I got shot down, the thing I've dreamed of most is coming here on a Sunday morning. When I woke up this morning, I knew I had to drive straight here to see you and Mom and Kansas."

Bob uncapped two beers and handed one to Stan. "I better call Dot and tell her to set another place for dinner."

"Don't do that Dad. Let's surprise her."

Bob walked around the counter and sat down next to his son. "Are you going back?"

"I've only got a few days leave."

"I thought so." Bob poured his beer slowly into the glass and watched it foam to the top. "You're a long way from Kansas."

"Hell Dad, I could fly in circles over Nebraska and Iowa just so long."

Bob looked at his beer glass and then looked at Stan and smiled. "At least I don't have to worry about you breaking every window in town and getting court-martialed."

That too had been a Sunday morning. A Boeing B-47 six-engine jet bomber flew over Mankato low enough to be easily heard. As it reached the edge of town the pilot wagged the wings back and forth. By now everyone was on their doorsteps watching as the big silver jet climbed slowly into the sun. Then it made a wide, graceful turn back toward the town. They watched as it grew larger and larger, sinking lower and lower, making no sound as it came closer and closer. Then it flashed overhead with a thunderous booming roar that made everyone duck in panic. The next day several people claimed their windows had been broken by the noise. The Air Force had investigated. Stan was a suspect as he had been flying a B-47 that day from Pease Air Force Base in Maine to Roswell, New Mexico.

"You're lucky no one got your tail number. Finish your beer and let's go."

"I'm in no hurry Dad. It might be a while before you and I can sit here and drink a beer on a quiet Sunday morning." Stan lifted his bottle toward his dad and held it until Bob raised his glass.

At last, they finished and Stan set his empty bottle down. He started to stand up but couldn't.

The pain in his leg made him gasp and he fell back into the muddy bottom of the bomb crater. Fighting against waves of pain, he pulled off his helmet, unbuckled the parachute harness and then dragged the parachute canopy down alongside in the mud. A small man wearing what looked like black pajamas and carrying an AK47 assault rifle appeared at the edge of the crater. The man stood silently without expression looking down at Stan.

A Shared Secret

This is a confession of sorts. I've never told anyone and never really expected that someday I would reveal everything that happened to me and what I did that night on the summer after my graduation from high school so long ago,.

My girlfriend, Barbara Mahoney, and I had planned to go to a friend's graduation party. Alas that plan was wrecked. Barbara called me the day before and told me she wasn't going with me and that she wouldn't be seeing me anymore. My world went black. I knew there was nothing I could do, no way to bring Barbara back. I went to the party anyway, said hello to the crowd and slunk away into the dark to brood over my fate. I was young enough to recover and that recovery was helped along by the story I'm telling you now.

A few days ago, I received a letter announcing the reunion of my High School graduation class. Along with the invitation was a list of class members who've "gone on ahead." I saw Barbara's name on the list. They're all dead now I thought; Barbara, Rosemary,

Tacy, Ellen and Jim Rossberg. Jim was four years older than me and he plays a part in this story.

As far as I know, Barbara never told anyone about what happened, at least no one ever mentioned anything about it and now I guess the story can be told.

The summer of my high school graduation I was working at the Oxford Standard Station on the west edge of Worthington. Interstate 90 didn't exist then, so US Highway 16 was the main tourist route across southern Minnesota; a steady stream of cars heading west and east were going right past the station. We were usually pretty busy pumping gas, fixing tires and selling bug screens. The station opened at 7 AM and closed by 10 PM. I usually opened up four mornings a week and closed up five times a week. I was saving money for college, so working long hours was okay by me and kept my mind off Barbara.

I remember the fateful night vividly; July 16. The sun set that night about 9:30PM and by about 10 o'clock only the last glow of twilight remained; I was standing in the doorway getting ready to shut off the gas pumps and turn off the outside lights when the Mahoney's big black Buick pulled onto the apron with Barbara behind the wheel. As the car stopped, Barb's head dropped between her arms and slumped over the steering wheel. I stepped outside and walked toward the car. Barbara didn't stir. I hesitated, waiting for her to make the first move and when she stayed still, I reached down and opened the car door. Barb raised her head slightly and turned toward me; her face was wet with tears and ashen with fright.

"Help me," she sobbed.

I didn't know what to say so I just held out my hand, pulled her out of the car and guided her to the bench in front of the station building, sat her down and sat next to her.

"What's wrong?"

"He was grabbing me, and I hit him." She inhaled slowly and put her hands over her face.

I reached up and pulled a hand away from her face. With the other hand still covering half her face she stared at me with the one tearful eye.

"I killed him," she whispered. "He's in the back seat."

"I'll call the police."

"No! No! I didn't mean it. Everyone will know. Won't you help me?"

"Okay, tell me exactly what happened." It never occurred to me to look in the back seat of her car to see if there really was a dead body. I needed to get her to calm down and then try to convince her to go the police. So, I asked her to start at the beginning and tell me what happened.

Barbara, and three of her friends were at the band concert at Chautauqua Park she said. It was so hot they decided to leave ahead of the crowd and go to Pratt's Ice Cream Parlor for an ice cream cone. Barb was driving her dad's car and Tacy her own car. Someone suggested going to the drive-in theater. When they arrived at Pratt's there were only a few people inside. The only ones they recognized were classmates, Mike Thompson and Lois Nau. Lois sometimes worked nights at Pratt's; her boyfriend, Leon Wiese was in the army, so she was okay working nights. None of the girls liked Mike so they just ignored him.

Barb ordered an ice cream cone and was paying for it when Tacy said she had decided to just go home, it was too hot to go to the drive-in. The other two agreed and said they were calling it a night too. Barbara told me she was a little ticked off but didn't much care except she didn't want to be left alone at Pratt's with Mike Thompson. As the four girls walked outside, Barb said she was going to drive around Lake Okabena to Slater Park, eat her cone and watch the sunset.

"Mike must have overheard me telling everyone where I was going. I drove out there, parked along the lake, got out and sat on the front fender, the sun was almost down, it was very still. I was just finishing my ice cream when Mike drove in behind me.”

Mike had a reputation as a rough guy and he ran around with a rough bunch that was avoided by the saddle shoe crowd, which included Barb and her friends. Barb said she was afraid of him.

Mike got out of his car and walked over to Barb, hopping up in the fender next to her. Feeling trapped, Barb didn’t move, and Mike did all the talking; asking her if she was still going out with me and wondering if she’d like to go out with him. Barb said she just shook her head. Then he put his arm around her. She tried to pull away, but he held her tight. He slid his free hand up her dress along her thigh. She struggled and pushed his hand, but he was too strong. Then he jumped off the fender, pulling her with him and shoved her to the back of her car. He jerked the back door open and pushed her onto the back seat and fell on top of her.

“I don’t know why I didn’t scream. I was paralyzed, I couldn’t think, I just wanted him to stop.”

She described wrestling him as he tore at her clothes and pulled down her patties. Somehow, he let go of an arm and she reached out to hit him. When her hand touched the floor by the seat, she felt something hard, grabbed it and swung as hard as she could.

“He went limp. I pushed him off and pulled myself out of the car. Then I started hitting him with my fists, but he didn't move at all. My dad plays horseshoes in a league and I grabbed one of his horseshoes from the floor of the back seat and that's what I hit Mike with. I didn't mean to kill him. I just wanted to run, so I drove the rest of the way around the lake. Will you help me?"

"Barbara, we've got to call the police otherwise you'll be in even more trouble." I was sure she'd make things worse by trying to avoid being found out.

Barb was convinced that I'd be able to get her out of this fix and nobody would ever know. Somehow, she got me to agree to help her and to get Mike's body out of her car. I think I was dreaming that I'd get her back.

The gas station had two service bays, so I drove the big black Buick into one and then drove my car into the other one. The shop lights were off leaving the service bays dark and the outside lights reflecting off the glass overhead doors would stop prying eyes from seeing what I was doing. I opened the back door of the Buick and pulled Mike's body out. Now all I had to do was get him into the trunk of my '39 Ford Coupe. Mike wasn't too big, but trying to lift and move a dead body isn't really a one-man job. I pulled, pushed and rolled until I got his head and arms over the bumper and into the trunk. Then I was able to lift his legs up enough to roll them into the trunk and get the lid closed. I was really sweating by the time I was done. I opened one service bay door and backed the Buick out, parking in the same spot where Barb stopped when she drove in. I was relieved that no customers stopped while I was wrestling with Mike.

Barb was still sitting on the bench where I left her. I went in the station and bought a bottle of Nesbit's orange from the pop machine, brought it out and handed it to her. She took a drink of the pop and smiled weakly at me. I sat down next to her, took her hand and shook my head.

"Barb, listen to me very carefully, what I'm going to tell you is really important because we're about to do something that will get us both in big trouble if we're ever found out." She nodded and took another sip of the orange pop.

"First, you've got to promise to never, ever tell anyone what you did tonight. No ifs, ands, or buts; do you understand? No friends, no parents, no one you think can keep a secret. Can you do that?"

She looked at me and nodded.

"If anyone asks about tonight, you have to tell them exactly what you did tonight; just leave out what happened with Mike. Otherwise, don't ever change a single detail. Don't ever leave anything out. Don't ever make anything up; always tell the exact truth. Do you understand?" I let go of her hand and squeezed her shoulder.

"Yes. I'll never, ever tell and I'll never let on that you helped me."

"There's one more thing you've got to make sure you get right." I paused to emphasize the importance to my question.

"Why did you come here to see me?" I knew that if anyone ever followed her path it would lead them here and she needed a good answer to that question. I guess I needed that answer too; she'd dumped me but came running as soon as she needed help.

"This part is true," she said. "I've felt sad about what I did to you and the way I broke it off. I didn't have the nerve to see you face to face, but I wanted to say I'm sorry for the way things worked out. Before Mike drove up, while I was eating my ice cream cone and watching the sunset, I decided that I'd see if you were working tonight and come over and face you and apologize. So that's the reason I came to you." She looked away for a moment and then stood up.

"What will you do with Mike?"

I said I hadn't figured that out yet but not to worry. I actually came up with a plan while I was putting Mike in the trunk of my car, but I wouldn't tell Barb, she mustn't ever know what I did so she could never slip up and get me dragged in.

"Go home. Tell your folks you saw me and you're feeling too low to talk. Take a bath and go to bed." I took her hand and walked her to the car. She squeezed my hand, got in her car, started it and drove away without looking back. I didn't know it then but that was the last time I'd ever talk to her. We showed up at the same place from time-to-time, even said hello, but we never actually talked beyond the hello and how are you. For some reason she never ever came to our high school class reunions even though she lived in St. Paul.

I turned off the outside lights; made sure the electricity was turned off to the gas pumps, took the money drawer out of the cash register and hid it under the pop machine, went into the service bay and grabbed a bundle of shop towels, opened the service bay door, got in my car and backed it out of the service bay, pulled the door down, locked the front door of the station, got in my car and headed east down Oxford street.

Worthington was growing and the city had built a new sewage treatment plant just north of town. The plant included two large settlement ponds surrounded by a chain link fence. A gravel track wound around the ponds with a locked gate at the far end. The ponds were far enough out of town that they were completely hidden by farm fields and tall weeds grew up on both sides of the track, tall enough to keep a car hidden. The summer before a few of us got a six pack of beer and decided that parking on that gravel track would be a good spot to avoid being caught while we sipped that forbidden brew. We broke the padlock on the gate and drove in by the ponds. Once we were next to the water, the smell was too much so we left and never came back. So that's where I headed; I was pretty sure I could drop Mike off there without being seen.

I turned off Oxford Street onto the gravel road leading to the treatment plant. Once I'd gone a short distance, I shut off my headlights, the rising moon gave me just enough light to see the road. When I spotted the gate, I stopped the car by pulling the hand brake so my brake lights wouldn't go on. I shut off the car, rolled down the window and sat for a few seconds. Nothing was stirring, totally quiet; no cars coming. I jumped out, ran to the trunk, opened it, pulled out the handle to my tire jack, closed the trunk lid and walked to the gate. I was going to use the jack handle to pry off the lock. When I reached for the padlock, I discovered that it had been pried open already. It could have been from our break-in a year earlier!

I pulled the gate open and sprinted back to my car, started it and drove onto the track. I stopped inside the gate, using the hand brake again; got out and closed the gate. I drove in far enough so my car wouldn't be visible from the road. I didn't use the hand brake but just shut off the motor and let the car coast to a stop. I undressed completely, socks, underwear, everything I had on. Leaving my clothes on the seat, I got out, closed the car door with just a soft click. Standing naked next to a sewage treatment pond in the middle of the night is a memory that still makes me shiver, but I didn't have time that night to stand out there in the dark shivering.

I opened the trunk and pulled Mike out. Then I dragged him off the track and into the pond. At night the water was black as ink. The bottom was soft, so I sank in as I pulled Mike out toward the middle of the pond. I kept wading out until I was waist deep then I let go of Mike. His body didn't really sink; it floated just beneath the surface. I waded back to the edge of the pond where the banks were lined with large rocks. I picked one that I could carry and waded back toward Mike. I had some trouble finding him in the dark water, but I finally bumped into a leg. I slipped the large rock under his shirt so it would stay on his chest and was glad to see him sink out of sight.

I waded back to the car, took the shop towels out and wiped myself off until I was completely dry. I threw the towels in the trunk, put on my clothes, started the car and backed slowly toward the gate. I opened the gate and backed onto the road. Leaving the car running, I ran to the gate closed it, made sure the padlock was in a position, so it looked like the gate was still locked, ran back to the car a drove away. I didn't turn the headlights on until I was close to the edge of town.

I got home about 11; Mom and Dad were in bed asleep. I decided that I smelled bad enough that I'd better take a shower. If I woke folks up, I'd tell them I spilled some gasoline in myself and need to clean off. They didn't wake up.

Worthington was quiet for a couple of days. An abandoned car at a city park took a few days to generate much excitement. We sometimes left our cars to go somewhere with friends and then couldn't remember where we'd left the car. Sometimes it took over a day to find the missing vehicle. So, a day passed before there was any effort to find Mike. The police and sheriff departments started a search. The volunteer fire department started dragging Lake Okabena around Slater Park. On the third day, the Worthington Daily Globe headlines proclaimed, "SEARCH FOR MISSING WHS GRAD UNDERWAY." The effort was intense but fruitless. The dragging stopped after 4 days. A couple of Boy Scout troops spent a week searching the shoreline for a mile in each direction from the park but didn't turn up anything. The Globe printed an appeal for anyone who had seen anything or had seen Mike on the day he disappeared to contact the sheriff's department. I later learned that Lois Nau was the only one to call.

Jim Rossberg was 4 years ahead of me in school. I think he went to Worthington Junior College for 2 years and then went to work for Sheriff Sandy Duehl as a deputy. Jim was a bright guy and a hard worker and, as the newest member of the department, he was given jobs no one really wanted to do. They gave him the task of gathering information on the disappearance of Mike Thompson.

A week after Mike disappeared; I was cleaning the windshield of a car I'd just filled up when a sheriff's car pulled into the station. I finished with windshield and went inside to ring up the sale.

Jim got out of the squad car and walked inside right behind me. I gave the customer his change and turned to Jim.

"Are you Gary Walters?" I think Jim knew who I was; he really got into being a deputy.

"Yes," I answered trying not to sound nervous.

"I'm investigating Mike Thompson's disappearance, and your name came up."

"Me? I haven't seen Mike since the night we graduated."

"Did Barbara Mahoney stop by here to see you around 10 o'clock last Tuesday?"

"Yes, I was getting ready to close up when she drove in."

"Why did she come to see you? What did she want?

I shook my head and looked down. "We used to go together. We broke up the day before graduation. She said she was feeling bad about that and wanted to come and apologize. We talked and we shared a bottle of pop and then she left." I raised my head and looked him in the eye, hoping I sounded convincing and that Barb and stuck to her story.

Jim asked a few more mostly meaningless questions. I guessed he was checking that Barb came to the station and when she got there.

At last Jim said thanks, got in his squad car and drove away. I hoped that was the end of it.

July faded into August. I worked hard but managed to take a few days off to go swimming at Lake Okoboji in Iowa with Leroy Nau and Jim Ulrich. I was also getting ready to leave for college at Mankato State. I planned to work right up until the day I left; I need all the money I could save for college.

"BODY FOUND AT SEWAGE PLANT," screamed the headline of Tuesday's Daily Globe. Every Monday, Bill Nyens drove out from the city garage to do a routine check out at the treatment plant. When he finished his work inside the plant, he usually drove the track around the ponds to make sure they were draining properly and everything was okay. Monday, August 13th proved to be his unlucky day as he spotted a tennis shoe with a foot in it sticking out above the water in the second pond. He raced back to the treatment plant, called the city garage, told them what he saw and asked them to call the sheriff. I guess there was quite a stampede to the sewage plant as word spread around town. There didn't seem to be any way they could connect me to the body in the pond, so I wasn't worried. I should have been.

It was a week later to the day when Deputy Rossberg drove up to the station. My boss, Bill O'Brien, was gone making his morning run to the bank so I was alone, and we were busy with tourist traffic. Jim parked his car and walked over to the pump island where I was filling up a station wagon loaded with baggage and kids.

"I've got a couple of questions to ask when you get a second." He turned away and walked into the station.

What now I thought. Did Barb blab after they found Mike's body? If she did, my goose was cooked. I finished filling up the station wagon, washed the windows and walked back to the station office where the tourist dad was standing next to the cash register with money in his hand. I rang up the sale, took his cash, counted out his change and pushed the cash drawer closed.

"Can we go back in the shop?" Jim asked as he walked from the office into the service area. Without turning he said, "Where do you keep your shop towels?"

I walked past him and pointed to a cardboard box on the work bench.

"The dirty ones are in pail next to the bench."

Jim walked over to the box, took one of the towels out and looked at it.

"Who do you get your shop towel service from?"

"United Uniform in Luverne; we get our uniforms from them too." I wondered where this was going to lead.

"Damn." Jim looked at the rag, sighed and then looked at me. "I thought we had a good piece of evidence. They picked up a shop towel by the sewage pond where the body was found. Turns out almost every garage and gas station in town uses United; even the city uses United. Now there's no way to tell where that rag came from. Your towels are even a different color, blue, and the one we found was brown." He handed the rag back to me, turned quickly, walked out, got in his car and left.

If Jim had looked in the dirty towel barrel, he'd have discovered it was full of brown towels. The laundry service stopped by every other Tuesday, picking up our dirty uniforms and shop towels and replacing them with clean ones. Sometimes the shop towels they left were blue, sometimes brown. The last batch we got were blue, I had escaped suspicion. When drying myself off that night I should have counted the towels I used to make sure I didn't leave one behind; I just picked up the wet ones and threw them in the car trunk and then buried them under dirty towels in the pail the next morning. I must have dropped one and didn't notice it in the dark.

I kept waiting for the other shoe to drop but there no more visits from Rossberg. The Daily Globe ran a story on how Thompson died. When they found the body, it was sent to a medical examiner in Minneapolis. The report said Thompson didn't drown; he was dead before his body went into the pond. The report also said the cause of death was a blow to the base of the skull which fractured his C2 neck vertebra, severed his spinal cord causing him to stop breathing. I think Barb grabbed the horseshoe in such a way that she hit him with the pointed open end of the shoe.

After that story there were no more updates on the investigation. I started packing to head for Mankato and the beginning of my college career; thoughts of Mike Thompson and Barb Mahoney had faded.

By the end of August, traffic on Highway 16 slowed and the station wasn't too busy. On Friday morning, August 31, Bill was in the front office getting a gasoline delivery order ready and I was in the shop mounting a set of new tires. I heard the phone ring but didn't pay much attention, nobody ever called me at the station.

"Gary, it's for you."

I walked into the office, puzzled about who would call me at work.

"Is this Gary Walters?"

I recognized Jim Rossberg's voice; he was being the deputy again. I told him it was me.

"Can you come down to the Sheriff's office we need to talk?"

My heart sank. Now what turned up? I couldn't think of anything that would drag me back into that sewage pond other than a slip up by Barbara. I told Bill that I was going out for lunch and would finish mounting the tires when I got back. I was pretty nervous on the drive downtown to the courthouse square. As I pulled up to park, I couldn't help noticing that the Sheriff's office and the county jail were both in the same building; that wasn't reassuring. Taking a deep breath, I got out of my car and walked up the office door. Jim was sitting at a desk at the back of the room; there was no one else there. He motioned me to a chair next to his desk. I sat down.

"I just got back from a week at the FBI Academy in Arlington, Virginia. Sheriff Duehl sent me to their course in criminal investigation. It was pretty good, and I learned a lot. I've worked on this Thompson murder for almost two months and never seem to get anywhere. Now I think I've discovered something, and I want to go over it with you."

Jim slid a blank sheet of paper over toward me, picked up a pencil and drew a long line across the paper. At the beginning of the line, he made a little tic mark and wrote 9:10 under it.

"That's when Barbara and her friends left Pratt's shop. Lois Nau is sure about the time. Barb's friends were also sure about the time.

Now he made another tic mark a little to the right of the first one. He wrote 9:20 under the new tic.

"I drove from Pratt's to Slater Park several times. It never took me more than 8 minutes, but we'll be a little generous and give Mahoney 10 minutes."

He then put a little tic mark at the very right end of the line and wrote 9:55 under it.

"Barbara Mahoney got to your station at that time, and you've confirmed that. It never took me more than 7 minutes to drive from Slater Park to your gas station, but I'll give her a minute extra."

He made another tic just to the left of the 9:55 one and wrote 9:45 under it.

"The question is what happened between 9:20 and 9:45. Here's what I know; Lois Nau said Mike Thompson left Pratt's a few minutes after Mahoney."

He made at tic and labeled it 9:12 then he made another and labeled it 9:22.

"Unless he stopped somewhere, he arrived at Slater Park around that time."

Now he made another tic between 9:45 and 9:55 and labeled it 9:50.

"Officer Wayne Redenbaugh was making a routine patrol around Lake Okabena that night and pulled into the driveway at Slater Park where he saw Thompson's car with the driver's door open and the keys in the ignition. He looked around a little but didn't find anyone. That's not too unusual because people often get out of their cars and walk around the park or go neck in the bushes. He called base on the radio and reported that he was leaving Slater Park and would check Sunset Park next. His call was logged at 9:52."

I could see where Jim was headed. There was that gap between 9:22 and 9:45; twenty-three minutes.

"Mahoney said no one was at the park when she got there, and no one was there when she left. We now have a couple of puzzles. Where was Mike Thompson between 9:22 and 9:45? If Mahoney left at 9:45 and Officer Redenbaugh got there at 9:50 how did Mike Thompson disappear in just five minutes and end up in a sewage pond ten miles away?"

Jim circled the blank interval between 9:22 and 9:45; put the pencil down and looked at me.

"I learned a lot about timelines at the FBI Academy. Once I plotted this out it I could see that there had to be another person involved. Here's what I think happened."

Jim explained his theory. Thompson followed Mahoney to Slater Park and attacked her. Someone else showed up, killed Thompson with a blow to the back of his head, took the body and dumped it in the sewage pond. Jim sat back in his chair and folded his hands behind his head and looked up at the ceiling.

"What do you know that you're not telling me? Was there someone with Mahoney when she came to the station? Did she tell you anything about what happened at Slater Park?"

"Jim, I've told you everything I know. Barb and I only talked about our breakup, and she was alone. She never even told me she was at Slater Park."

"Does she have a new boyfriend? Did he help her?"

I said I didn't know anything about a new boyfriend.

"Is she lying? How do I know that you didn't close the station early and go meet her at the park? Can anyone verify that you were at the station until ten?"

"Arvin Whelan drove in on his motorcycle and bought a couple of buck's worth of gas and was driving away just as Barb drove up. I'm sure he'll remember that."

Rossberg looked down at his timeline diagram and shook his head. I'll bet getting me to Slater Park in time to kill Mike Thompson was the only plausible solution he had left. It never occurred to him that Barb could have killed Mike. It never occurred to him that Barbara had Mike's body in her car when she came to see me. It never occurred to him that the shop towel tied me to the sewage pond and connected me to Mike's body. I didn't dare ask him what Barbara had told him; I didn't want to start him down a new path now that he was so lost on the one he was on.

The interview was over, and I left the Sheriff's office, went back to the station and finished mounting the tires. The next Tuesday I loaded my car with everything I had and drove to Mankato. I didn't look back.

When I came back for our 60th class reunion, I drove around Worthington looking at familiar landmarks. Pratt's Ice Cream Parlor only lasted a few years, but the store front is still the same. Interstate 90 north of town now carries all the tourist traffic, so Obie's Standard Station on Oxford Street is long gone. The sewage treatment plant has been expanded along with bigger settlement ponds. Slater Park hasn't changed a bit; even the same old wooden sign is still there. I didn't bring up the Thompson Murder Mystery at the reunion and nobody else did either, so I guess it's pretty well forgotten.

As far as I know, Barbara never said anything to anyone. When she mentioned her new boyfriend to Rossberg she must have given him an ironclad alibi. So, I'm the only one who knows.

I wonder though. While on a short visit to Worthington, I picked up a copy of the Worthington Daily Globe newspaper and took it with me. A few days ago, I was idly leafing through the newspaper when a story caught my eye. The city had hired a new female police detective, and the article described one of her initial assignments was to review case files on old unsolved serious crimes. The first thought to come to mind was the shop towel I'd dropped at the sewage ponds. If they still have it, would they test it to see if my DNA is on it? I wonder.

Night Route

Walt lived his entire life in New York City, most of it on Manhattan Island, more specifically on the Upper East Side of Manhattan and now at 240 93rd Street, Apartment 1421. Walt and his wife Ellie bought the co-op apartment when he retired in 2023 from the New York Transit Authority after driving a New York City bus for forty-one years. Ellie retired as a lab technician from the New York City Sanitation Department that same year.

For forty-one years he'd gotten up at five AM, slipped behind the wheel of his bus at six AM to start his route, the M20. To many, driving a bus over the same fixed route for seven hours a day, five days a week would seem mindlessly boring. In fact, Walt loved his routine. He recognized almost every person who boarded. Many talked to him and shared quick stories about their lives. Even those who never talked were welcomed aboard with a smile and usually even smiled back. Most passengers sat in the same seat every time they boarded. If someone was missing for a few days, they were welcomed back with relief and expressions of concern. The regulars were like a family. At Christmas time Walt puts a box of chocolates next to the coin box. He used to wear a fake nose on Halloween until the Transit Authority adopted a policy against costumes.

Once in a while someone would step on board and whisper to Walt that they had no money for the fare. Walt would explain that he could not let anyone aboard without paying the fare. As he explained this rule, he would take a five-dollar bill, and a one-day bus pass out of his pocket and smilingly tell the surprised passenger that just this once the ride was on Walt.

A man got on one morning and pulled a gun demanding money. Walt explained that the fare box was locked and hard to pry open, but he could try while Walt waited for the police that he'd called with the silent alarm. The robber thought better of the idea and got off the bus. Walt did not let on that he had the key and there was no silent alarm.

There were a few emergencies. A passenger's sudden heart attack had Walt wheeling the bus into the emergency entrance of a hospital, luckily only two blocks away. The other passengers quickly got the man off the bus into the emergency room. A woman rider who knew the man said she'd stay with him to make sure his wife would get contacted. Walt boasted later that he was only five minutes behind schedule when he got back on his route. He also boasted that he'd never had a traffic accident except for the drunk who rear-ended him while he was letting someone off at a bus stop.

After his final run on his last day of work Walt parked his bus at the garage and sat glumly in the driver's seat. He waited almost a minute to switch off the engine. Before he could compose his thoughts on what lay ahead, the shift supervisor pulled open the bus doors and jumped aboard.

"Walt, you son-of-gun; you did it! Now the world's your oyster! No more driving in circles with a bunch of grumpy passengers. Get up and get in the ready room for your retirement celebration."

The was no escaping his send-off. Walt knew his co-workers meant well and he wanted to say goodbye, but his heart wasn't in it. To tell the truth he was terrified of not having the comfort of his daily routine. Now all he wanted to do was to steal away and go home. He climbed out of his driver's seat for the last time, stepped out of the bus, threaded his way through the rows of parked buses, went inside the office and strode into the ready room. The other drivers cheered, crowded around him, shaking his hand and shouting congratulations. He did his duty, smiled and thanked everyone for the retirement gifts they eagerly presented to him, an engraved desk clock and an expensive suitcase. He ate as much cake as he could and drank a glass of lemonade. He'd turned in his driver's ID card and they gave him a one-day pass and two transfers, which he used to ride home.

"What now" rolled over and over through his mind as he looked forlornly out the bus window at the passing traffic.

Ellie met him at the apartment door, threw her arms around him and gave him a big kiss. He gave her a long hug.

"Are you up to going out for dinner?"

Walt almost said no but he knew if he gave in to the remorse of losing his purpose in life he'd struggle forever.

"Let's go the Greek joint over on first. I'm ready for some lamb and I'll bet you can get your favorite — scallops!"

The restaurant was crowded but not too noisy so Walt and Ellie were able to talk without shouting. Ellie ordered wine and Walt ordered scotch and water. They sat silently for a few moments.

"Tell me everything" Ellie said as she reached over a placed her hand on Walt's wrist.

Walt looked at Ellie and shook his head. "I'm lost. Today I was a bus driver; tomorrow morning I'm nothing. What will I do?"

"Take me to Paris. Let's go to Coney Island. Tomorrow morning let's have breakfast at the Bagel Joint and take the subway downtown and go up the Empire State Building."

Walt gave her a weak smile and leaned over planting a kiss on her cheek.

"That's not what I mean. We'll do everything we've talked about and more. I've worked all my life; I need to feel needed; I need to be of use to someone besides you."

They lingered over their lamb and scallops. Ellie had another glass of wine and Walt another Scotch. Together they planned a full day of sightseeing to celebrate Walt's first day of retirement; Empire State Building, walk across the Brooklyn Bridge, ferry ride to the Statue of Liberty and Ellis Island and visit to the 9/11 Memorial. They held hands as they walked back to their apartment.

During their long careers Walt and Ellie both worked hard, lived modestly, and invested their savings in retirement programs. They tried but never had any children and finally let that phase of their life together pass. They became the quintessential New Yorkers; almost never venturing out of the city, making friends in the apartment building they lived in, riding buses and subways, never owning a car, going to Coney Island on summer holiday, Rockefeller Center for Christmas.

Every night he'd gone to bed at nine thirty and quickly went to sleep. Now he'd usually lay awake well past midnight, so he started staying up watching TV, doing crossword puzzles or reading but that only made getting to sleep harder. Finally, he started going for night walks. The upper east side is dominated by tall apartment buildings so the sun usually disappears in late afternoon leaving slowly deepening twilight and early darkness. After dark the east-west streets become nearly empty and quiet while the north-south avenues, particularly First and Second Avenues, remained busy, lit up with small shops, cafes, bodegas and bistros. During Walt's early night forays, he sometimes walked up Second Avenue, but the pedestrian traffic annoyed him, so he stopped going over there; using Fifth, then Fourth and ending up back on Third Avenue. Then he started walking to a bench on the 93rd Third Street intersection across from Second Avenue.

Walt liked the bench and started ending his walk every night there. After a few days sitting alone on the bench an older man walked over and sat down next to him. Walt nodded but didn't say anything. The man pulled a pack of cigarettes out of a shirt pocket, drew one out, lit it, took a long drag and exhaled.

"My mother was a dancer when she was young." The old man spoke without looking at Walt. He took another drag on his cigarette. "She was beautiful and a very good Latin dancer. She often danced with Rudolph Valentino. Nightclubs would pay her to be a partner with Valentino. I think she was eighteen or nineteen then." He sat in silence slowly smoking his cigarette. Finally, he dropped the cigarette butt and ground it out with his foot; stood up and walked away into the dark.

Walt watched him disappear and realized that he had enjoyed the small encounter. He stood up and walked back to the apartment relaxed and ready for a good night's sleep.

Without realizing it, Walt gradually modified his late evening walking routine. After he watched the evening news he went to the kitchen and buttered two slices of bread, wrapped them in waxed paper and slipped them into his pocket. He walked over to Ellie, gave her a kiss and headed for the door.

"I'll be home by eleven."

Walt followed his usual route; he walked over to Lexington Avenue then down to Eighty Fifth Street and over to Fourth Avenue. He glanced at his watch as he started up Fourth. He was a couple of minutes behind schedule, so he picked up his pace. By the time he reached 96th Street he was right on time, but he decided to keep his faster pace as he crossed over toward Second Avenue where the heavy pedestrian traffic often slowed him down. He kept the pace and soon arrived at 93rd Street and Second Avenue. He smiled as he settled into his seat on the 93rd Street bench at exactly ten o'clock. He was just taking his first bite of the bread sandwich when a familiar figure dropped onto the bench beside him.

"You know Walt, I'll bet you were always on time when you drove a bus."

"I never want my passengers have to wait." Walt smiled then took another bite.

Like riders from Walt's past, they slipped out of the darkness, climbed aboard the bench, rode awhile and then stepped off leaving room for Walt's next passenger. Promptly at ten forty-five, Walt got up and started home, his shift over. He hummed softly to himself as he walked up 93rd contented that he'd completed another shift on his night route.

Missteps in Vermont

There are many outdoor enthusiasts who enjoy hiking. Among that group are those who are drawn to the challenge of routes classed as difficult or challenging. Many of those routes are found in mountainous terrain. usually defined by steep, rocky trails with uneven footing, narrow passages and vertical sections requiring use of hands as well as feet. Embarking on a day hike on one of those trails requires pre-planning, attention to proper equipment, and adherence to safety procedures. One of the rewards of hiking those trails is the personal satisfaction of completing a difficult endeavor and enjoying being immersed in a beautiful landscape. The Green Mountains of Vermont offer hikers many opportunities to satisfy their desire to conquer difficult and challenging trails.

Mount Mansfield, Vermont's highest peak at 4,385 feet is twenty or so miles northwest of Burlington, Vermont's largest City. One of the most popular outdoor recreation destinations in New England, the mountain is home to skiing, snowmobiling and hiking.

Mansfield has hiking trails of every length and degree of difficulty; something for everyone.

Roger Ackerman enjoys the out-of-doors. He and his wife Susan hike and ski often. They use the Mount Mansfield trails, enjoying the exercise and the scenery, every chance they get.

Burlington, Vermont looks swept clean on this late October morning. The city sparkles in the clear air; to the northeast, the Green Mountains shimmer in gold, red and orange. Roger stepped onto his back deck, drew a deep breath and looked northeast to Mansfield Mountain. Fall in Vermont; blue skies, sunshine, balmy and windless, trees clothed in dazzling bright colors. A truly lovely day for late October. Susan is working all day, so Roger decided he'd go up to Underhill Park on the mountain and hike up to the Sunset Ridge Trail; thinking it might be his last chance at such beautiful weather!

He called Susan on his cell phone and told her he was going hiking at Mansfield Mountain on the Sunset Ridge Trail and expected to be back before she got home. His next move should have been to call the Weather Bureau to get a forecast for conditions at Mount Mansfield. He decided to use his computer instead of calling. Without thinking, he set his phone on the counter and headed toward his office. As he passed the hall closet, he stopped, opened the closet door, reached in and pulled out his hiking backpack, switching his focus to checking the contents of the backpack; he turned into the bedroom where he could spread the contents on the bed for an inventory.

A seasoned hiker, Roger kept his backpack well stocked with necessities; a light windbreaker, sweater, stocking cap, first aid kit with fire starting essentials, fifty feet of light rope, flashlight with a headband, compass, and a large plastic bag for emergency shelter. Usually there was also a pair of leather gloves, but he'd worn them to trim bushes the other day and forgot to put them back in the pack. He'd pick them up when he got to the car. The warm weather caused him to set his hiking boats aside and pull-on lightweight climbing shoes instead. He then went to the kitchen where he grabbed a couple of energy bars and a full water bottle and added them to the pack.

Roger looked at his watch and decided he'd better hurry if he was going to be home when Susan got back. He scribbled a note reminding Susan that he'd gone hiking at Underhill State Park and should be home by 5PM, grabbed his backpack and a hiking pole, jumped in his car and took off.

Twenty minutes later Roger stood in the Underhill Parking lot admiring the vibrant fall colors blanketing Mansfield Mountain. It was Monday so the nearly empty lot didn't register. On a summer weekday the lot would be nearly full by noon. He looked at his watch, settled his pack, took a firm grip on his hiking pole, and started up the Halfway House Trail to Sunset Ridge. The two trails hiked in sequence make a six-mile loop that climbs twenty-four-hundred-feet up the east side of the mountain in the three-mile outbound leg, topping out on a ridge overlooking the western slope. The steepness of the climb and the rocky footing give the trail a rating of "Difficult." and slow, the average pace is 1.5 miles-per-hour. The descending downward leg on Sunset Ridge is three miles long through a series of switchbacks to the trailhead parking lot. A seasoned hiker can easily make the loop in less than four hours. Roger started up twenty minutes after noon, so he expected to be back at his car well before 5 o'clock sunset.

Halfway House Trail is popular and well maintained, but the foot path is rocky and uneven. The uphill climb is a steady steep grade climbing 2,400 feet. Roger set himself a moderate pace and planned to stop for a short rest at the shelter where the trail jointed Sunset ridge and started downhill. He did pause a few times to survey the lovely fall colors of the mountain and the valley below.

Hiking upward, the trail is sheltered behind the ridge over the western slope of the mountain. Below the ridge the air is still and the temperature warm even at the increasing altitude. As Roger crested the ridge-top exposing the long western flank of the mountain he now felt a brisk cold wind from the northwest and with it a sharp drop in temperature. The sun was barely above a dark bank of clouds now sweeping up the mountain toward him. Startled, Roger realized he'd forgotten to check the weather. He also realized his cell phone was on the kitchen table.

For a second, he started to panic but quickly focused on a mantra he'd often evoked, "if you've got time to panic, you've got time to find a solution to your problem." He turned back to the trail and started downhill along Sunset Ridge without asking himself if there was any way to shorten his descent. The downhill leg of the trail is almost all on the western slope of the mountain, so Roger was going to be in the wind and the cold and whatever the dark clouds were bringing.

The downhill trail is a series of switchbacks to mitigate the steep descent. At the first switchback there's a small trailside shelter. Roger gratefully stepped out of the wind and opened his backpack. He pulled his windbreaker and stocking cap out of his backpack, put them on and then discovered that his gloves were missing. He shrugged dejectedly, fished his extra pair of socks out of the pack and pulled them on his hands. As he pulled his pack back on, the sun slipped behind the clouds, and he saw the first few flakes of snow swirling around the shelter; big flakes that quickly melted as they touched the ground.

The downward trail is exposed to the wind, The jumble of rocks piled alongside trail lets the snow swirl down and drop on the trail. Because the day was warm the snow quickly melted leaving everything wet and slippery. Roger knew he'd have to move slower to make sure he wouldn't lose his footing. By now the heavy clouds covering the sun darkened the sky making it hard to follow the trail in the snow swirling flat light. Treacherous footing, flat light and blowing snow hampered Roger's pace. The wet snow was quickly soaking his light climbing shoes and he felt his toes getting cold. A couple of times he discovered he'd wandered off the trail. This unnerved him. He looked at his watch. Time was flying by and hiking a wet and now muddy and steep mountain trail in the dark would be almost impossible even with a flashlight. Roger started using his walking stick like a blind man's cane; sweeping it side to side to alert him if he strayed off the trail. It was slow going as Roger felt his way downward.

The Sunset Ridge Trail is often over large slabs of smooth granite, poor footing, slippery when wet and dangerously slippery when snow covered. The wind breaker and the sweater weren't heavy enough to blunt the cold, so roger stopped, pulled the large plastic bag from his pack, cut slits in the top for his arms and a hole for his head and pulled in on. The ersatz poncho would keep him dryer and provide extra protection from the wind. He felt around in his pack and found the flashlight and headband, pulled it on and turned on the light.

At one point the trail disappeared into a dark downward chasm. Roger sat down and slid his feet onto a large rock to brace himself. He carefully and slowly edged downward, sliding cautiously from one rock to another. He used this technique several times to negotiate the steepest parts of the route.

Slowly, he crept downward, edging his way along what seemed to be endless twists and turns. It seemed to Roger that he was no nearer the bottom than when he started down. Then his light caught a sign with an arrow pointing to the Underhill Parking Lot. He'd reached the bottom of the Sunset Ridge Trail and could now relax on the gentler Underhill Parking Lot Road. He was soaking wet with sweat, his feet seemed like lumps of ice, his pants were muddy, and his fingers were cold and stiff inside his wet sock gloves. He felt relieved, even buoyed by a sense of accomplishment. The one mile walk to his car would be a breeze!

At twenty minutes after five Roger knew he was at the bottom of the trail; but where was he exactly? The trail ended in a series of parking lots which were not lighted. The snowfall ended only to be replaced by mist and heavy fog which obscured everything; how would he find his car? If I head straight west, he thought, I'll come to highway 108 but that's a long hike. Roger pulled off the plastic bag, unzipped his windbreaker and slid his frozen hands under his armpits.

He stood warming his hands and feeling his feet freeze. Then he reached into his pocket and pulled out his car keys.

"I wonder how close I have to be to my car for this to work?"

He pushed the panic button on the key fob and listened. Silence. Using his compass, he walked west for ten minutes and tried again. This time he thought he heard a horn honking. He walked for five minutes and tried again. This time he heard the horn and saw his car lights flash.

He almost ran to the car. Opening the back, he threw in his backpack, stripped off his wind breaker and sweat soaked sweater. Opening the driver's door, he pulled down his muddy pants sat on the driver's seat and took off his muddy shoes and pulled the wet socks off his frozen feet. He then slid out of his pants and pulled himself into the car. He started the engine and sat shivering while it warmed up. Once the heater breathed warm air, he turned the fan up to max, put the car in gear and headed home.

In the comfort of his car, Roger pondered his missteps; he didn't check the weather forecast, he didn't carefully inventory his backpack, he didn't take his cell phone, He didn't turn around when it started to snow taking a more sheltered and shorter route down. He was careless but lucky.

It was after six when he drove up his driveway. At the sound of the car pulling into the garage, the kitchen door opened, Susan, whooping with delight, ran out to the car.

"God, I'm glad to see you! Are you okay?" She shouted.

Roger opened the car door and stepped out, nearly naked, barefoot, wearing only a tee shirt, and baggy wet underwear. Susan took one look and shrieked with laughter. She pointed at him, held her hands over her face, doubled over consumed with mirth, staggered to Roger, kissed him and then continued to laugh.

Once inside, Susan called the sheriff and let them know Roger was home safe. Roger took a hot shower while Susan sat in the kitchen still laughing.

Primrose Tales

These few short stories are my attempt to bring back to life the memories of her childhood given to me by my mother, Lillian Dewey McCauley. As far back as I can recall I was regaled by stories about her early years in Primrose, a small rural Nebraska town located in Boone County. My grandfather, George Laurin Dewey, was a doctor who came to Primrose with his new bride in 1906 and practiced medicine there until 1923 when the family moved to Cedar Rapids, Nebraska. Dr. Dewey and his wife, Lillian Pearl Russell Dewey, raised five children; G. Gordon, Mable Mae (called Mibs), Dorothy (called Dot), Lillian (called Lal) and Marjorie (called Marge).

The Deweys are buried in Rose Hill Cemetery in the town of Albion, Nebraska, the county seat of Boone County. Their plot also includes the grave of a daughter, Geraldine, who died shortly after she was born. There is also a headstone for their son, Gordon, although I'm not sure if he's buried there. There are no longer any surviving members of that family. My Aunt Marjorie, the youngest of the Dewey children, died in March 2008.

These stories are not in themselves true, but are based upon incidents related by my mother that were worthy of weaving into a short story. The reader will note that the leading characters are the members of the Dewey family. It seemed to me only fitting that they be allowed to return to play themselves and give us an opportunity to hear their voices once again. All of the other characters are fictional with some exceptions. Aunt Mibs told me that friend of hers always was the maid, Chaucy, whenever they played house, so she re-appears in "<u>Hollyhocks</u>." Wherever I could, I used the names of real people such as Sheriff Anderson, the banker, Mr. Primrose, and the livery stable owner, Mr. Snodgrass that I gleaned from historical records.

Dr. Dewey, my grandfather was always referred to as "Daddy" and his wife, Lillian Pearl, as "Mother." I've used that convention throughout these stories as it seemed to be a natural way to blend my voice with that of the storyteller.

These stories are generally set about 1918-1922. My mother was born on January 15, 1914, and was the fourth youngest. The population of Primrose at that time was about 200. Its small size meant it lagged in things like electricity and long-distance telephone service. In researching elements of the history of Primrose, I discovered an interesting coincidence. In the story "A CARTWHEEL FOR SKEETER" you will note that the banker's name is Primrose. The Primrose family were early members of the community, and the village may have been named after their family. Other sources indicate it was named after the flower.

Today little of Primrose remains. The Great Depression and the coming of the automobile moved commerce to the County Seat, Albion, about 15 miles northeast and Cedar Rapids, about 8 miles southeast. It is interesting to note that there is a Dewey Street in Primrose, which, I believe was named after our family.

Snowfall

Thickening clouds dimmed the wintery afternoon light, fading colors, reducing everything in the snow-covered landscape to shades of gray. Even though there was no wind and it hadn't as yet grown particularly cold, the homeward-bound schoolchildren walked quickly and silently, their heads bent into collars and scarves. Lamplight already glowed from a few windows foretelling the gathering darkness.

Gordon got home first. He quickly pulled off his coat, leaving mittens in the sleeves, hung it carelessly on the coat rack and ran upstairs to his room. The noise of his footsteps had barely vanished when Dorothy and Mabel Mae burst through the door with gasps of relief from the cold. Dorothy opened her mouth to yell out a greeting when she noticed the sliding doors to the front room were closed. She nodded to Mabel Mae and rolled her eyes, the two of them took off their coats in silence. On cold days Daddy sometimes saw patients in the front room rather than at his office next door. He said it was too hard trying to keep the office warm.

Mother was darning socks in the kitchen; she looked up over her glasses as the girls strolled in.

"Gordon is writing a horror story. It's called The Red Spot," Mabel Mae exclaimed.

"He's going to read it to us tonight. He says we won't be able to sleep in the dark ever again," Dorothy added breathlessly.

"I'm sure you won't." Mother smiled. "Why don't you two go upstairs and do your homework before it gets dark. Daddy is seeing patients here today."

The girls turned in unison and started for the stairs.

"Maybe he's got old man Walker in there," whispered Dorothy.

"Oh pew!" Mabel Mae held her nose.

Dorothy giggled.

Mr. Walker often sought out Daddy to treat his "irregularity". One-time, next door at the office thank God, Daddy had given him a "high enema". Mr. Walker was draped face down over the examining table while a concoction of warm water and Epsom salts was administered into the recalcitrant orifice. Daddy instructed him to hold tight until he was seated on a chamber pot. The warm salt water was such an effective stimulant that Mr. Walker never even had a chance to stand up before the resulting eruption sprayed far and wide. Mabel Mae and Dorothy were given the unpleasant task of cleaning up. They both claimed afterward that Mr. Walker hit every medicine bottle and jar in the office!

As the girls disappeared upstairs, the front room doors slid open and a man stepped into the hall, pulled on his coat and was gone into the gray cold. Daddy came out next and walked back to the kitchen.

"I think that's the last one for today. Looks like it's getting colder, the front windows are frosting over." He gave Mother's shoulder a squeeze. "I'll have Gordon bring up some coke from the cellar."

"We're having meatloaf for supper so have him get a bunch of carrots too."

Daddy called Gordon down and then went back into the front room and emptied the last of the coke briquettes into the hopper on top of the stove. By the time Gordon came downstairs Daddy was waiting at the bottom of the steps with the empty coal scuttle.

Gordon lit a lantern and climbed down the steep stairway and ducked into the musty low-ceilinged cellar. The far wall gleamed with orderly rows of glass canning jars - peas, beans, corn, plums, pears, peaches, apples and pickles. On the floor stood a large, covered crock full of sauerkraut. Two gunny sacks full of potatoes sat under the stairs and next to them a shallow box full of sand. Gordon filled the scuttle from a sack of coke in the coal bin and then went over to the box full of sand. He dug away until a fat carrot emerged. Grasping it he pulled the whole bunch free. He brushed the sand off and dropped them on the coke.

"The red spot travels at night. It glows in the dark and slides along the floor - under doors; it seeps through cracks and hides behind curtains." Gordon moved the lantern and watched the shadows slide in menacing patterns along the walls. He smiled as the story played out in his mind just like a movie.

"Gordon! Have you decided to live down there?"

At the sound of Mother's voice, he picked up the coal scuttle and climbed back into the kitchen. He handed the carrots to Mother and took the scuttle of coke into the front room and set it by the stove.

"Tell the girls to come down and help with supper."

Gordon bounded back up the stairs to his room.

Daddy pulled the front room curtains back, looked out through the frosty window and watched as a man climbed out of a wagon and walked up toward the house. Just as the stranger raised his hand to knock Daddy opened the door.

"Afternoon Doctor."

"Come on in. Get out of the cold." Daddy stood aside, let the man inside and quickly pushed the door shut behind him. "What can I do for you?"

"I'm Ed Summers, a neighbor to the Overdahls. Her baby's com'n and Lyle asked me to fetch you."

"Ed, take off your coat and warm up a bit. Come on out to the kitchen." Daddy grabbed an arm and led Ed to the kitchen.

"Lillian, meet Ed Summers. Ed, this is my wife, Lillian. These two girls are my daughters, Dorothy and Mabel Mae."

"Pleased to meet'cha. Sorry to bust in like this, but Mrs. Overdahl is having her baby, and I came for the doctor."

"Well Mr. Summers, I'll tell you what we're going to do. You sit here, have some hot coffee and warm up. I'll go out and hitch up the sleigh and follow you back to the farm. That way when I'm done you won't have to drive me back to town." Daddy pulled a sweater over his shirt, put on his fur cap and a wool coat.

"If we get going, we'll be out there before it gets too dark. I'll be right back, enjoy your coffee." He opened the back door and was gone.

Before Mr. Summers finished his coffee, Daddy stomped back in. He took off the wool coat and hung it up by the door, and then he took off his shoes and carried them into the hall and returned wearing a pair of heavy boots, carrying his black bag and an enormous fur coat.

Daddy went over to the cellar door, opened it, reached inside and took out a lantern. "I've got to put some kerosene in the lantern and then I'll meet you out front."

Mr. Summers stood up, put on his coat and cap and pulled on his mittens. By the time he opened the front door, the sleigh was pulling up behind the wagon. Ed pulled the door shut behind him, strode over to the wagon, patted his horse, climbed onto the seat, clucked, slapped the reins and they were off.

Daddy liked the sleigh in winter. When the ground froze, he could go straight across the fields, which always seemed quicker and easier than grinding along a rutted road. He often chose a route that took him past his favorite hunting places. On house calls out in the country he often carried a gun, a rifle in the winter and a shotgun the rest of the year. If he'd been alone today, he would be looking for jackrabbits and have the gun across his lap. The fur cap was pulled far down on his head and the collar of the great fur coat was turned up and pulled around covering his face, still the cold air bit at the end of his nose and made his eyes water. A dark hairy buffalo robe covered his legs.

There was no twilight; it simply grew steadily darker as they rode slowly northward. Primrose faded behind the snow-covered hills, leaving the cold, silent, empty vastness of the rolling prairie surrounding the wagon and sleigh, dwarfing them both into two tiny black specks crawling silently across a grey featureless plain.

Finally, Mr. Summers stopped, climbed down off his wagon and hurried back to the sleigh.

"You can see their place on the left, at the top of the hill. I hope everything goes well with Mrs. Overdahl." He raised a mitten in a goodbye salute as he turned back toward the wagon.

Daddy watched as the wagon swung off the road onto a faint track leading downward into a grove of trees, waving goodbye in return.

As the sleigh pulled into the farmyard the kitchen door opened and a large man carrying a lantern stepped onto the porch. Behind him in the doorway crowded the three Overdahl children.

"Even'n Doctor Dewey. Cold night for a drive."

"It sure is Lyle." Daddy pulled off the buffalo robe and swung down, shaking himself like a great bear in his fur coat.

"Well go on in. The misses knows you're here. I'll unhitch the horse and put him in the barn."

Lyle Overdahl was big, pink skinned with light blond hair and bright blue eyes. His arms were great round posts and his hands were thick with fingers like sausages, his barrel chest and smooth round stomach seemed to stretch his skin tight. He was a gentle and jovial man, always friendly, always laughing.

The damp warmth of the kitchen made Daddy realize how cold his face had become. He set down his bag and pulled off his heavy mittens. The two Overdahl daughters each grabbed a mitten and stood impatiently awaiting the next article to be shed. They both looked like their father - large, pink, blond and bright blue eyed. Like their father they were also gregarious and cheerful.

"Mom's having a baby."

"Silly, he knows that he's the doctor."

"I know that."

"My name's Frieda. I'm nine years old."

"I'm Pauline and I'm seven."

"Nice to meet you both. How's your mother?" Daddy pulled off his coat, gave it to Frieda, who staggered to a chair and draped it over the back.

"She went to lie down." Pauline took Daddy's hat and put it on top of the coat.

Daddy took his bag and went through the front room into the bedroom, the two girls trooping along behind.

Jenny Overdahl was sitting up in her bed, bundled up against the cold. Her dark hair was let down, framing a slender face and dark eyes. She smiled shyly as Daddy walked in and set his bag down on the nightstand. Alongside the bed stood Jon, the youngest of the three Overdahl children. Jon was dark and shy like his mother. As Daddy approached the bed Jon slid down on his haunches until only the top of his head appeared over the far side of the bed.

"Eve'n Doctor. Sorry to get you away so late in the day."

"I'm glad I got here in time, Jenny. Don't trouble yourself about the time of day. How are things going?" Daddy sat down on the edge of the bed.

"The pains aren't too bad. I don't think it will be too long now though. I'm so big it must be another girl. Oh!" She took a quick breath and put her hands down on the bed, grabbing at the quilt.

"Children, I have to look at your mother so all of you go back to the kitchen. When we're done you can come back."

Daddy got up, ushered them out and pushed the door shut. This was Jenny's sixth delivery, so he knew she understood what was happening.

"The water broke about an hour ago. I wish it would be a boy. I'd like another boy. There's towels on the chest when we need them, and I put a full kettle of water on the stove."

About that time things started to happen fast, and the door stayed shut. Once the baby's head appeared the rest was easy and soon Daddy held a big, blond-haired, beet red baby boy in his hands. He smiled at Jenny and winked. Lifting the baby by its feet he put a finger in its mouth to make sure the airway was open and then he gave at a light slap on the buttocks. True to the obvious heritage, the boy didn't cry; he grunted and then started to breathe. Daddy tied and cut the cord, wrapped a flannel blanket around the squirming infant and handed him to Jenny.

"Jenny, you've got a boy, and he looks just like Lyle. I'm going to clean you up and then let everyone have a look at him." He helped Jenny finish, cleaned up the bed and pulled the covers back over her.

As Daddy pulled the door open, Frieda and Pauline jumped up and ran across the room, Lyle's face brightened when he saw Daddy's broad smile. Even Jon forgot his shyness and ran over to get a good look.

"We're going to give this big boy a bath."

"Yea! a brother!" Frieda jerked Pauline's arm.

"Just what we all wanted!" Pauline jumped up and down, clapping her hands.

Lyle put the dishpan on the table and partially filled it from the kettle on the stove.

"Just like last time, Doctor. I'll make it just warm enough." Lyle stuck a finger in the dishpan to check its temperature. He added a dipper of cold water and tested again.

Daddy unwrapped the baby and gently lowered him into the bath.

"Frieda and Pauline, I want each of you to bring me a towel. Jon, go into your mother's room and fetch my black bag.

The three children tumbled into the bedroom and returned with their equipment.

"Frieda, put your towel on the table. Good. Pauline, when I put the baby on the towel, you cover him up with yours."

Daddy lifted the baby out of the bath and put him down and Pauline covered him up. Daddy dried him off.

"Jon, let's have that bag and we'll make sure your new brother is OK."

Daddy opened the bag and proceeded to examine the baby while the wide-eyed gallery watched every move.

"He's fine and now it's your mother's turn."

Daddy brought the baby back to Jenny. She already had him nursing by the time Daddy finished re-packing his bag. Jenny smiled contentedly, first at the baby and then at Daddy.

Lyle insisted that Daddy have something to eat before he left, putting a big bowl of bean soup and a slice of bread on the table. If he could avoid it, Daddy never ate farm food. He worried that the lack of sanitation meant too many chances for illness. Sometimes, he just had to accept the kindness.

After Daddy finished eating, Lyle poured them each a glass of home-made elderberry wine and they drank a toast to the new son. At last Lyle went out to hitch up the horse and Daddy put on his coat and hat and mittens and lit his lantern.

Daddy hung the lantern on a hook in front of the sleigh, climbed aboard and pulled the buffalo robe around his legs.

"Bring Jenny and the baby in to see me in four days. Thanks for the soup." Daddy held out a mittened hand and Lyle pumped it with bone crushing sincerity.

"My mind rested easy when I saw you come up the road. I didn't think you'd get here in time. Have a safe trip home." Lyle stepped back and Daddy flipped the reins.

Soon the darkness of night surrounded the lonely sleigh, flickering lantern shadows quickly disappearing into the gloom, making it seem as though the world ended at the dim circle of lantern light. The sleigh lurched and skidded on the rutted track; Daddy hunched down into his coat and pulled the robe tighter around his legs.

Softly, downy flakes began to glide into the lantern light. A few at first, slowly, gently, dreamily wandering into the golden circle, languorously falling onto the track. Then the few swirled onto a thickening cloud that dimmed the lantern light and frosted the horse in feathery white. The sleigh began to glide silently as the fresh snow covered the track and the horse's hoof beats faded until only the muffled jangle of the harness broke the stillness.

Daddy strained against the swirling lantern light and the snowfall quiet. As if entranced, his eyelids grew heavy, the reins drooped, he slowly sank deeper into the upturned collar of the great fur coat and the snowfall's stillness claimed him.

The ringing seemed far away, but he couldn't tell, maybe it was close. Was it across the river? He could see the river shining through the great chestnut trees. The early morning sun and the mist over the river surrounded him with a soft, golden light. What was the ringing sound? No, it wasn't ringing at all; it was the blacksmith, pounding on his heavy anvil, the bell-like notes echoing through the Connecticut hills and over the Ten Mile River. If he turned around, he would see the house and barn and Lebanon Town. He wondered if he should run home and tell mother that he heard the blacksmith. The golden mist drifted toward him until the trees disappeared.

Daddy's head nodded slowly deeper into the collar of the fur coat, and he smiled faintly at the boyhood vision that took him back. The harness jangled musically to the rhythmic motion of the horse. The golden circle of lantern light moved slowly through the falling snow, an eye of light peering into the winter solitude, watching upward toward the nodding, snow covered figure huddled in the sleigh.

He felt a lurch and reached up for a leather strap to steady himself as the rocking streetcar slowed, the conductor kept ringing the bell. The trees were festooned with long grey-green wisps of Spanish moss and the hot, humid New Orleans air made it hard for him to breath. In the waiting crowd he could see his brother Dumont's dark curly hair. Dumont smiled and then held up his arm and waved. He smiled back. He wanted to wave but kept his grip on the leather strap. How different New Orleans was from New England, from the forest covered hills and the neat farms with their stone fences. Dumont's face seemed to float above the crowd.

Under the dark bowl of night, the horse plodded onward, now a ghost-like figure, draped in a white snow-mantle. The sleigh glided along behind, masked in blue-black snow shadow that made it appear empty, as though its occupant had drifted away into the falling snow.

It wasn't Dumont's face at all; in fact, he couldn't see any familiar face on the crowded platform. The train had almost stopped, steam hissed softly around the passenger car and the engine bell clanged. He stood in the open doorway, the cool rain brushing against his face. The sign on the depot said "LEIGH, NEBRASKA". He took a deep breath, the air smelled crisp and clean. The crowd of faces smiled up at him through the rain.

Daddy wiped a snow-covered mitten over his face. The sleigh stood still, suspended in the cavern of darkness. In the snow-filled lantern light he couldn't see beyond the horse. Throwing off the buffalo robe he climbed down from the sleigh, sinking up to his knees in the soft snow. Taking the lantern off its hook he waded toward the horse's head. Holding the lantern high with one hand, he grabbed the harness with the other and saw why they'd stopped.

"I don't know how you do it." Daddy let go of the harness and rubbed the horse's nose. He reached out and slid the barn door open. They are home.

Hoxie Meets His Match

Commerce Street slid quietly into the afternoon, dinner was over, and the shadows had started creeping over the board sidewalks and into the dusty gravel, the bustle and noise of morning fading into the fluttering chatter of sparrows dusting themselves in the street. Storekeepers on the shady side of the street came out and cranked up their canvas awnings while their counterparts in the sunny side cranked theirs down.

Lillian sat where she often did in the afternoon, on the office step in the shade. The office was right next door to the Dewey house and both buildings faced east onto Commerce Street, but Lillian preferred the office step. She sat with her arms wrapped around her drawn-up knees, rocking slowly back and forth on the step, dreamily watching what little activity there was on the nearly empty street and waiting for Daddy to come back to the office.

As Lillian watched, a team of horses, driven by Hoxie Boyce, jangled around the corner and clopped slowly up the street.

The team stopped in front of Ward Snodgrass' livery stable, and Hoxie swung down from the wagon. Tall, lean, lose-limbed, big-eared, big-nosed with watery pale-blue eyes, Hoxie is always easy to spot and even easier to hear; his loud voice booms over Primrose whenever he is in town. When he speaks his voice crashes like a whole stack of plates hitting the kitchen floor and thumps like a thousand potatoes being dumped down the basement steps and grates like chalk on slate. Hoxie Boyce almost never has anything important to say; still, he talks often and loudly.

Hoxie tied the reins to a wagon wheel and disappeared into the blackness of the stable doorway.

"AFTERNOON." Hoxie's disembodied greeting echoed out into the street like a rock thrown against a metal shed.

Lillian stopped rocking and let go of her knees. She could see Daddy walking up the other side of the street toward the livery stable. He was wearing a vest and white shirt, but his tie and celluloid collar had vanished, victims of the summer afternoon.

Even without the black doctor's bag you could tell Daddy was a professional man. He walked erect and purposefully, greeting the storekeepers with a cheerful wave or a nod and smile as he passed. As he drew alongside the livery stable Hoxie appeared in the doorway.

"HI THERE DOC. HOW'S BUSINESS?" Hoxie poked Daddy's bag with a long bony finger and smiled broadly.

Daddy gritted his teeth and managed a wan smile in return. Daddy hated being called doc; to him it was at best crude slang and at worst a coarse insult. He was a doctor, a learned man, a healer, a person whose profession deserved respect. His friends called him George, his family called him Daddy and everyone else should at least be civilized enough to call him Doctor.

Hoxie, ever blissfully ignorant, held his hand out and Daddy shook it perfunctorily.

"Good afternoon, Hoxie. Having trouble with one of your horses?"

"GINGER'S FAVORING A LEG. FIGURED I'D BETTER GET IT LOOKED AFTER. SLOW DAY ANYWAY." Hoxie sent a stream of brown tobacco juice into the dusty street to punctuate the end of his statement. A single amber droplet glistened on his lower lip. "IF I WAIT TOO LONG, SHE MAY BE RUINED FOR GOOD."

"I think that's a" Daddy started to say "wise course" but caught himself in mid-sentence. "Prudent decision." Nothing could bring Daddy to use the word "wise" when it was directed at Hoxie. Fearing that

Hoxie would ask him to examine the ailing horse, Daddy quickly stepped off the sidewalk into the street, avoiding the area where Hoxie's ejection had landed.

"MAYBE YOU SHOULD TAKE A LOOK AT HER, DOC?" Hoxie laughed and slapped his leg.

Daddy just shook his head and kept walking.

Lillian jumped up as Daddy crossed the street toward her.

"Is there anything you need me to do, Daddy?" Lillian liked to help Daddy in his office.

"Well thank you Lillian, darling. Did anyone come by while I was away?" Daddy took Lillian's hand as they strolled across the wooden sidewalk toward the office.

Lillian shook her head.

"Let's go inside and see what needs to be done." Daddy pulled his key chain out, slid his hand to the end where a single brass key hung, put the key in the lock, twisted and pushed the office door open.

The front room had three wooden chairs along one wall and a large roll-top desk flanked by glass-fronted bookcases along the other. Over the desk hung a large, framed diploma stating that the Regents of Tulane University had proudly awarded George Laurin Dewey the Degree of Doctor of Medicine and all the rights and privileges there-to. Except for a doorway leading to the examining room and a small stove, the far wall was bare. Daddy walked through the front room and into the examining room.

Two large west windows filled the room with sunlight making the row of white cabinets along the near wall glisten. A long black examining table angled across one side and a dentist's chair faced it from the other. Behind the chair was a linoleum counter with cupboards underneath. On the countertop sat a basin and pitcher. Across the room the wall was lined with shelves of medicines, salves, ointments and pills arrayed in colored bottles of every shape and size.

Daddy set his bag on the dentist's chair.

"Lillian, don't ever take up with a man that chews tobacco. It's a disgusting and unhealthy habit".

"Why do they do it then? Does it taste good like candy?"

"No. In fact, it will make you very, very sick if you swallow it; you get cramps and diarrhea. Men who chew tobacco are too ignorant to do anything else. Honey, I need some fresh water." Daddy filled the basin and handed the empty pitcher to Lillian.

Lillian had just returned after filling the pitcher from the backyard pump when the front door of the office burst open with a bang.

"Come quick! Hoxie got kicked by a horse and I think he's dead!" One of Ward Snodgrass's sons, red faced, wide eyed and out of breath stood gasping in the doorway.

Daddy grabbed his bag off the chair, hurried out the door and headed across the street. Lillian put the pitcher down and followed.

Light from the wide doorway quickly faded into the dusty cavern of the livery stable. Horses shifted and snorted in their stalls; the air was heavy with dust and the pungent aromas of liniment, leather and manure. As Daddy's eyes accustomed themselves to the gloom, he could see Hoxie lying face down in the dirt in an alleyway between the stalls. Daddy quickly knelt down and slid his hand under Hoxie's neck, feeling for a pulse. Lillian stood beside him watching. Daddy's hand was covered with blood when he pulled it back.

"He's alive; knocked unconscious by the kick. Lillian, go to the office and get a package of cotton and that pitcher full of water. Ward, have you got a blanket or something we can roll him onto?"

Daddy stood up and wiped his bloody hand on his handkerchief.

Ward brought a horse blanket and spread it out alongside Hoxie.

"He'd just finished unharnessing her. Damnedest thing, tripped on a harness strap as he was walking behind. She nailed him right there. I guess he must have startled her."

"We've got to turn him over. I'm going to hold his head while you boys roll him onto the blanket. I don't think his neck is broken, but we can't be too careful." Daddy knelt down at Hoxie's head and cradled it in his hands.

Ward and his son slowly lifted and rolled Hoxie onto the blanket. His eyes were open and full of dirt; blood bubbled from split lips and ran from his nose. His lower jaw sagged limply to one side. Lillian came back with the cotton and the pitcher of water.

Daddy carefully cleaned Hoxie's face with cotton dipped in water. Using a wad of cotton like a sponge, he squeezed water into the dirt filled eyes, gently coaxing them clean. Hoxie lay motionless.

"Is he dead?" Lillian asked softly.

"No. You can see him breathing; watch his chest go up and down. He's unconscious, but I think he'll come to before too long. Looks like his jaw is broken, but his nose seems okay."

"Let's carry him over to the office. Ward, you and your son get on either side of the blanket, Lillian you hold his feet, and I'll take the head. We'll just walk him right across the street."

By now a small crowd had gathered outside the livery stable. When Hoxie emerged on his horse blanket bier, bloody and mangled, the crowd gasped and parted. Someone asked if he was dead.

"He's knocked out, but he'll live," answered Lillian trying hard to sound grown up.

They eased him through the office door and carried him into the examining room, laying him out on the long black examining table.

"Ward, can you send your son out to tell Hoxie's wife what happened and that he's going to be okay? I've got some work to do on his jaw, but he should be up and about by the time she gets here.

As soon as Ward and his son left, Daddy went to work. After strapping Hoxie's legs and arms down to the table, he took a large brown bottle of peroxide off the shelf, soaked balls of cotton with it and finished cleaning the bloody lips. Hoxie moaned at the sting of the peroxide.

"Hoxie, can you hear me?"

Hoxie moaned and his head moved a little.

"Good Fellow. You got kicked by your horse and your jaw's broken. I'm going to set it and wire your mouth shut. If the pain gets too bad, I'll give you a shot of morphine."

Hoxie groaned softly.

Daddy put his left hand on Hoxie's head and took the jaw with his right. Hoxie stiffened and wheezed as Daddy twisted the right side of the jaw.

"Dislocated and broken. Just one break, right on the chin. You're lucky. Not even a broken tooth." Daddy started slipping pieces of wire around Hoxie's teeth.

Daddy repeated the procedure on the other side of Hoxie's face. As consciousness returned, Hoxie's moans and groans grew louder as Daddy started to tighten the wires. At last Daddy was satisfied that the jaw was in place and the broken halves properly aligned.

"Now we've got to wire it up snug. This won't hurt too much. I've clamped wire around your teeth and now I'm going to twist them together tight to hold your jaw in place."

Daddy's hands were strong and nimble. Though he wasn't a dentist, occasionally patients came in to have a tooth pulled. Most of the time he could extract a tooth by the force of his squeeze on the extraction pliers; he more or less just popped the tooth right out. Now his fingers worked surely and steadily as he twisted the wires clamping the lower jaw tightly against the upper.

"I'm done. In three weeks or so and you'll be good as new." Daddy stepped back to admire his work. He liked what he saw; Hoxie's jaw had pulled together evenly. "I don't think I've ever done a better job of wiring a jaw. It looks perfect."

Hoxie was fully awake now and his eyes followed Daddy's every move. Lillian helped loosen the straps and Daddy eased the patient into a sitting position. Hoxie was pale and sweating, his jaw was starting to swell and turn black, both lips were puffed up and a bloody drool seeped from the corners of his mouth. He sat quietly, head down, breathing deeply and steadily.

Then he gagged, just a little. Daddy looked at him.

"Everything all right?"

Hoxie's head jerked up and his eyes widened with fright. He started to hiss and gurgle through his teeth. Daddy reached for his scissors. If Hoxie vomited with his jaw wired shut, he could strangle if the wires weren't cut.

Hoxie managed a long slow breath through his nose. You could see he was working his tongue furiously inside his mouth. At last, he exhaled and then took another deep breath through his nose. Daddy now stood directly in front of Hoxie ready to start cutting away the wires.

"Doc." Hoxie's voice grunted in a hoarse whisper through clenched teeth. "Eeee Doc. I got a chaw o tobacco in my mouth." Hoxie looked at Daddy with pleading eyes.

George Laurin Dewey, Doctor of Medicine, looked coldly at his patient. He had used all his skills and training to relieve pain and suffering, to restore health and vigor, to reconnect the broken and dislocated. For this he was just a "doc". He could just as well have fixed Hoxie's horse rather than his jaw. Although Hoxie didn't know it, he was going to suffer for his use of this casual appellation.

Daddy put his scissors back on the tray, walked over to the counter, poured water from the pitcher into the basin, slowly washed his hands and dried them on a towel.

Hoxie watched silently, puzzling about what was going to happen next and feeling the clot of tobacco in his mouth seeming to grow larger and larger.

Daddy put the towel down on the counter, turned around, and looked at Hoxie. He wore a sober expression and spoke in a deep and somber tone. "There's nothing I can do now. You'll just have to swallow it."

In a few weeks Hoxie talked as loudly as ever and he slapped Daddy on the back whenever they met and called him "THE BEST DAMNED DOC IN TOWN", laughing wildly and slapping his knee at his threadbare joke, Daddy being the only doctor in Primrose.

Daddy still bristled at "doc" but always gave Hoxie a knowing smile. It is nowhere recorded what the outcome of Hoxie's ingestion was; we do know that Hoxie no longer chewed tobacco.

Monday's Secret

Harry pushed and pulled with a steady rhythm, occasionally using just one hand when he took the big blue handkerchief out of his overalls to wipe the sweat from his face. The washing machine groaned and sloshed in reply to Harry's steady beat.

"We'll be done before anyone else is even started." Opal picked a wet sheet out of the basket and carefully pinned it to the clothesline. She smiled in self-satisfaction and gave a knowing look to Harry.

"I'm glad we'll finish before it gets hot. You'd think everyone would start early on a day like today. They'll sweat plenty for those extra minutes in bed. Better to get up and get going I say." Harry pulled out the blue handkerchief, mopped his face again and exhaled with a loud puff.

Mibs pulled the sheet up over her head trying to blot out the thumping and sloshing on the porch next door. "Five O'clock! Those old coots started washing at five o'clock." Mibs put her hands over her ears, shook her head and then pulled down the sheet, sat straight up and looked menacingly at the clock which now showed a few minutes before seven.

"Our wash is done! We're the first! No one ever gets theirs out before us! I'd like to take Harry and that fat old sister of his and stick them in that dumb old washing machine of theirs."

"Who are you talking to?" Lillian rolled over and looked sleepily at Mibs. "Harry and Opal wash and you talk to yourself. It's too noisy to sleep."

"It's time to get up anyway. By the time we finish breakfast they'll be done so we can help Mother without those two staring at us like we were monkeys in a cage." Mibs leaned over to the curtain, pulled it back until she could see through to the back porch next door; Opal was hanging up another sheet. Mibs stuck out her tongue as she let go of the curtain.

Mother already had the copper wash boiler heating on the kerosene stove when the girls brought their bed clothes down. They dropped the bundles on the back porch and went back to the kitchen. Cold breakfast on Monday mornings in the summer, too hot to start the cook stove and the kerosene stove is heating wash water.

"Where's Daddy?" Lillian asked.

"Delivering Mrs. Oltman's baby. He left about three."

"Oh shoot. I wanted to go along and help. Daddy said I could go. Why didn't he wake me up?"

"Lillian, there'll be other times. I guess he thought it was too early to get you up and drag you along." Mother gave Lillian's shoulder a soft squeeze. "He should be home soon. Hurry up and finish your breakfast we've got a lot of laundry."

"Doesn't Dorothy have to help? Just because she can sleep through a cyclone, we have to do laundry by ourselves." Mibs looked up at the ceiling as though she expected her sister, Dorothy, to fall through and land on the table.

"She'll be down before we're finished. There's enough to go around."

Lillian helped Mother sort the laundry into piles. Mibs pumped water out of the cistern and filled rinse tubs.

"Harry says it'll be a scorcher again today. I'm surprised you didn't get going earlier." Opal stood next door, admiring her laundry festooned porch.

"We'll be done soon enough," answered Mother.

"I used a different bluing and see how white the sheets and pillowcases are."

"They look nice." Mother answered looking up briefly.

Mibs poured a pail of water into a rinse tub and leaned over to Lillian. "I hope she falls off the porch and lands on her fat butt," she whispered.

"Mibs, for shame; what a way to talk." Mother shook her finger at Mibs, but a twinkle in her eye gave her away.

Lillian giggled.

Harry walked slowly back toward the house swinging two empty pails. "Those peas and beans are going to grow today. It's going to be a scorcher. I'm glad we're done." He held up the empty pails to ensure that everyone knew he'd poured the last of the rinse water on the garden.

Mother carefully ladled out hot water into the washing machine. When it was full she took the grater and began to shave a bar of soap into the steaming water.

"How nice to have soft rainwater. I hope we get enough rain to keep the cistern full all summer."

Mibs and Lillian took turns pushing and pulling on the agitator. Mother had to crank the clothes through the wringer, the girls weren't strong enough. Everyone took turns hanging out the wet laundry.

Opal and Harry cleaned out their washing machine, washed out the rinse tubs and hung them up; all the time scanning the neighborhood back porches, as though they were the official Primrose Laundry Police, carefully noting every fault.

"She doesn't care how crooked those sheets hang."

"Why do they let those lines get so slack, his trousers almost touch the ground?"

"Her whites are all yellow.

"It's ten o'clock and she hasn't even started.

Mibs and Lillian rolled their eyes as they listened. There was no escaping Opal and Harry and their laundry chronicles.

"Once, just once, I'd like to wash clothes in peace." Mibs looked at Lillian and shook her head slowly with disgusted resignation.

"Maybe they'll move away."

"Oh Lillian, what a nice thought. When you get bigger you'll move away, but Opal and Harry will be here all summer."

"We could pretend that they moved away."

Mibs put the last clothes pin on a cotton dress, stopped and looked at Lillian. She started to grin and then her eyes narrowed malevolently.

"Can you keep a secret?"

Lillian nodded solemnly.

Mibs cupped her hand over Lillian's ear and whispered.

Lillian's eyes widened as she listened.

"Will you help?" Mibs said at last.

"Yes. Yes. Let's do it."

On Tuesday Lillian went with Daddy to Columbus to visit patients in the hospital. They took the train and were gone all day. Dorothy had to scrub the kitchen because she slept through the laundry on Monday.

On Wednesday Gordon, Mibs and Dorothy went to a Methodist Church Social and Picnic at Albion. Only older girls and boys went so Lillian had to stay home.

It didn't rain all week. Each day was clear and hot, or as Harry loudly proclaimed, "Another scorcher". The peas and beans grew fast.

Daddy killed an old hen on Sunday and Mother made stewed chicken with mashed potatoes and fresh garden peas. They had the last jar of peaches for dessert. It was Dorothy's night to do dishes.

As Mibs carried the last plates over to the sink she looked at Lillian. "Are you ready?"

"Yes. Yes. Let's do it."

"Try not to make a big mess in the kitchen." Mother smiled and looked over the top of her glasses at the two girls.

"We'll be very, very careful not to spill."

"You two are crazy." Dorothy put on an apron and started on the dishes.

As the sun sank and the evening twilight slowly faded, Mibs and Lillian toiled in the kitchen, scrubbing and rinsing and squeezing. When at last they finished the sky was jet black and glittering with stars. The two sisters walked out on the porch and stood quietly, side by side, looking up at the night sky.

"I like this better than having them move away."

"Me too."

The dawn was only a grey promise when Lillian felt Mibs shaking her.

"Come on; let's get it done before those old coots wake up."

"What if they're already up?"

Mibs pulled a dress over her nightgown and Lillian put on a pair of overalls. They tiptoed, barefoot down stairs.

"Walk next to the side so the steps won't squeak so much." Mibs whispered as she stepped slowly downward into the gloom.

"What if they're up?"

"Lillian if you say that again you'll be sorry."

Furtively the barefoot girls carried their loads out to the back porch. As they worked they watched for any sign of life next door. Each time a bird chirped or dog barked or a floorboard creaked they froze like criminals caught in the act.

At last it was done. The birds were singing wildly and the dawn was pink with new life. The girls crept quietly upstairs and slid back into bed.

"Try to stay awake, Lillian. It won't be long now."

They watched silently, cautiously pushing the curtain aside, hoping for some activity in the house next door.

"There!" whispered Mibs. "A light. They're up."

A pump wheezed and gurgled. Pails clanked and the back door banged. Harry strode onto the porch and took the rinse tubs down from their pegs and set them on the wash bench. He struck a match and lit the kerosene stove. Turning he disappeared inside to the bang of the screen door.

"He didn't see anything!" Mibs hissed. "He must be going blind."

Opal came out carrying a white enamel pot. She climbed down off the porch, walked slowly to the outhouse and disappeared inside.

"Come on out you old biddy! Open your eyes!" Mibs shook the curtains.

Lillian crowded over to the window. "Maybe they're pretending not to see."

"Just wait. Just wait. When they look up - Oh boy!"

The outhouse door opened slowly -- part way and then stopped. Mibs grabbed Lillian by the arm and shook her excitedly. Then the door opened all the way.

Opal backed out, stood up, picked up the pot and turned around. She took one step and then she saw. The pot hit the ground with a clang, the lid clattering noisily alongside. Opal stood still for a long time, looking at the porch.

"Opal? What's the matter?" Harry's voice echoed through the screen door.

Snapped out of her trance, Opal grabbed the pot, put the lid on with cymbal-like crash and walked quickly up to the house, stamped up the steps and disappeared inside with a slam.

Mibs and Lillian squealed silently, shaking with glee.

"I thought she was going to faint."

"She woke up everyone in the neighborhood when she dropped the pot."

"Wait, here comes Harry."

Harry walked out on the porch and stood holding the screen door open as he looked next door.

Every sheet was hung just so, perfectly straight, dresses where lined up by size, socks hung in ranks, at attention like soldiers at West Point, shirts and trousers alternated with business-like uniformity. Never had laundry been hung with such attention to detail.

Harry and Opal washed clothes silently and shamefaced, casting sidelong and painful glances at the triumph next door. When they were finished they quickly disappeared back inside.

Mother said that since the laundry was already done and the kerosene stove was available they'd have waffles and syrup for breakfast. It's a good thing Opal dropped that pot or Dorothy might have slept right through breakfast.

A Cartwheel for Skeeter

Leaning his bicycle against the side of the depot building, Gordon walked out on the empty platform, stopped and looked down at the railroad track toward Cedar Rapids. Gordon was early and he knew it, the afternoon freight train from Spalding to Columbus had long since passed and the passenger train from Columbus wasn't due until three-thirty. What drew Gordon to the station was the "special" he knew was due this afternoon.

Strolling slowly along the edge of the platform, head down, Gordon studied the rails and ties and wondered if he put his ear on the rail, he could hear a train coming. Kneeling down, he reached out and touched a rail.

"Gordon, you're early." Station Master Jim McGlinchy stood in the depot doorway with his hands in his pockets. "The Special just left Belgrade and won't be here for thirty-five minutes. Come on in and listen to the telegraph."

Gordon often came down to the depot and watched the Station Master. Bright, inquisitive and curious; Gordon roamed Primrose, watching everything and asking questions. Questions which seemed far advanced for a twelve-year-old boy. Many adults, Jim McGlinchy among them, had grown used to the dark-haired, dark eyed, slender boy who would watch quietly and then pose often difficult to answer questions.

Jim turned and walked back into the depot. Gordon quickly jumped up and followed him in. Unlike depots in larger towns, this one is a cramped, single room with a small stove in one corner and a single bench for waiting travelers. A large desk faced a window that looked out on the platform and a narrow table separated the desk from the open waiting area. Occupying the center of the desk, a telegraph set forced neat stacks of freight bills, timetables and rate books aside, giving the Station Master unencumbered access to the telegraph key.

A telephone box hangs on the wall between the window and the door. This is more than an ordinary telephone, because it's connected directly to the Belgrade Telephone Company which has a long-distance connection. Anyone in Primrose needing to communicate with the outside world must come to the depot where they have the choice of sending a

Western Union Telegram or arranging a long-distance telephone call. Telegrams are the norm as considerable effort, cost and wait goes into getting through to your far-away party over the telephone.

Jim stepped between the table and desk, swung his chair round and sat down facing Gordon. "Grab that chair over by the stove and sit next to me. There should be some traffic on the wire any time now."

Gordon pulled the chair over and sat quietly. Within seconds the telegraph clattered to life.

"Cedar Rapids," said Jim. "Special should arrive there at two fifty." Reaching into his vest pocket, Jim retrieved his pocket watch, flipped open the cover, glanced at the time, closed the cover with a snap and deftly dropped it back into the pocket. "Should be here in thirty-two minutes I reckon, two fifty-three."

The telegraph clattered again.

"Spalding. The Motor departing at four forty-five."

Each day, a single-car, gasoline engine powered passenger train made a round-trip from Columbus to Spalding and back. Called "The Motor," it passed through Primrose at five P.M. on its afternoon run from Spalding back to Columbus. The Special would be safely on a siding before the Motor and the afternoon passenger train came through Primrose.

"Well, there's Ward with the horses." Jim stood up, pushed his way past Gordon and walked out the door. Gordon followed him onto the platform.

Three teams of horses clattered along the far side of the railroad tracks and swung to a halt across from the depot. Ward Snodgrass dropped the reins of the lead team and walked across the tracks to the platform.

"Afternoon Jim; train on time?"

"Train's due in at two fifty-three. They'll back it up the loading platform. You boy's will have to watch out for the Motor and the afternoon train from Columbus that'll be coming by while you're getting those engines off."

"Same as last year. It shouldn't take us more than an hour to get'm off if those monkeys know their job."

Gordon walked out of the depot over to a high-wheeled Railway Express baggage cart that sat in the shade at the end of the building. He hopped up on the cart and sat cross-legged ready to observe the all the action.

The Great War had driven wheat prices higher than ever, and farmers were planting wheat "fence to fence" to take advantage on this bonanza. The farms around Primrose were mostly too small to afford the expensive threshing machines and the steam tractors that powered them, relying instead on custom threshing contractors. Each summer during the wheat harvest, crews of men, steam engines and threshing machines move northward from Texas, through Oklahoma, Kansas, Nebraska, the Dakotas and Canada with the ripening wheat. Now it was Nebraska's turn. They sweep into a farm town like Primrose, fan out across the neatly shocked fields and swiftly strip them clean, thresh the wheat and depart for the next town north leaving behind straw stacks and mountains of burlap bags bulging with wheat.

The hilly terrain and small fields in Boone County meant the big threshing outfits swung west, leaving the area to the smaller outfits like the one arriving by train that would hopscotch from one small island of wheat to another.

Gordon sat fidgeting anxiously, waiting for the arrival of the threshing gang and their machinery. Soon the yellow glow of a headlight and a bonnet of smoke signaled the approaching train. With deliberate swiftness, the engine and its string of flatcars eased by the station and stopped just as the caboose came alongside the siding switch. The Brakeman swung down from the Caboose and pulled the lever to disconnect the caboose from the train. That done, he raised his arm signaling the Engineer to pull forward and leave the disconnected caboose behind. Once the last flatcar cleared the switch, the Conductor signaled again, stopping the train. He then threw the switch and signaled the Engineer to back the train onto the siding. The train backed slowly onto the siding until the last car nestled against the unloading platform. The Conductor and Engineer uncoupled the flatcars and a single passenger car, retrieved the caboose and backed it and engine onto the siding, clearing the track for the Motor and the local train.

As the flatcars stopped, men crowded out of the passenger car, scampering down the line of cars, clambering up onto the machinery, some grabbing planks, securing them in the gaps between the cars while others began unhooking the chains that held the giant machines in place.

A big, burly man strode purposefully along the cars, a slouch hat pulled low over his forehead and his thumbs stuck under his suspenders just above his belt. Otto Grien is head of this crew; he is BOSS and everyone knows it. By the time he reached the car next to the loading platform, Ward had a team of horses in place and was ready to hook a chain to the first steam tractor so they could pull it off the flatcar. Otto looked at the progress on the platform and scowled.

"Get a-goin we ain't got all day," Otto bellowed to no one in particular, punctuating his exclamation with a stream of tobacco juice.

With planks in place over the gaps between the cars and everything unchained and ready to move, the crew now turned to the steam tractors. Each tractor is manned by an engineer and his "monkey." The engineer is responsible for operating the tractor, regulating the boiler fire, maintaining steam pressure in the boiler and keeping the water level in the boiler high enough. His monkey feeds fuel into the firebox, keeps the feed water tank full and lubricates the shafts and bearings on the steam engine.

When threshing, boilers are often fueled with wheat straw, but here in town the monkeys are stoking the fire boxes with wood and coal. Soon a haze of acrid smoke envelopes the train yard. With the fires going, the monkeys run forward to help roll the first big threshing machine far enough forward so Ward and his boys can hook it up to the horses and pull it off. Within a few minutes the remaining tractors will have enough steam pressure to move under their own power. Each tractor is then hooked to the threshing machine behind it and slowly lumbers forward down the line of flatcars and off the loading platform. Last off are two water wagons and a supply wagon.

"You've got fifteen minutes to get across the tracks. The Local's due in at three thirty-eight," Jim McGlinchy shouts to Otto.

The Local train chugs through on time. With no passengers for Primrose or freight to collect, it slows down but does not stop.

All the threshing machinery is across the tracks and ready to move through town when the Motor signals its arrival with two metallic blats from its air horn. Gordon knows he may have to leave his perch on the baggage cart if anyone is going to unload anything from the Motor, but he sits and waits. The machine grumbles and squeaks to stop. Jim McGlinchy walks onto the platform, but no one gets off. A Railway Express man leans out over the half open door on the front end of the Motor but makes no move to indicate that there's anything to unload. Reverend Bader walks out of the depot toward the Motor, spying Gordon, he nods slightly and smiles. During his sermon Sunday morning at the First Methodist Church, Reverend Bader announced that he was going to Columbus for a ministerial conference and would be gone for two days. He quickly climbs aboard and with two short toots, the Motor, engine rumbling noisily, pulls away and is quickly lost from view.

The parade of equipment now began to move slowly forward, each of the four mighty steam engines pulling a threshing machine and the horse teams bringing up the rear pulling the water wagons and the supply wagon. As the procession turns up Commerce Street, people begin to gather in front of the bank. Jumping down off his perch, Gordon hopped on his bicycle and peddled toward the bank.

Migrant threshing crews most often were housed in the spare rooms in town, giving locals a little extra spending money and the crews a decent place to stay. The gathering crowd at the bank waited to meet their new boarders. Mr. Primrose, the bank president, stepped into the street holding a sheaf of housing assignment papers he'd collected from the crowd. Otto walked over to the banker, shook his hand and took the papers. He quickly started calling out the names on each paper. As a name was called, one of the crowd stepped forward. Otto then looked across the street at the crew. Almost instantly, one of the men stepped forward to meet their host for the next few days.

"Dewey," Otto shouted.

Mother held up her hand, walked forward and Gordon pushed his bike up alongside her.

Across the street, a young man stepped down from an engine and looked around to see if anyone challenged him. Smiling slightly, he strode toward Mother and Gordon.

"Hello ma'am, my name is Terrance McCarron. Most people call me Terry." He took off his cap and nodded to Mother.

"My name is Lillian Dewey and this is my son Gordon." Mother put her hand on Gordon's head and smiled back at Terry. "We're pleased to have you for a few days. Our house is right down the street. You can see it, right across from the livery stable." Mother pointed to the Dewey house.

"Yes Ma'am, Mrs. Dewey, I see it. Pleased to meet you, Gordon." Terry held his hand out and Gordon reached out and shook it. "I guess we're headed west for a couple of miles to our first farm. Once we get the machines set up we'll be back in town. About two hours I guess."

"I'm sorry my husband wasn't able to meet you. He's a doctor and is away on a call right now. Your room is ready and we'll wait supper until you're back."

"What do you do?" Gordon asked.

"I'm a monkey," said Terry.

"McCarron!" Otto stood on the supply wagon with his hands on his hips, frowning. "This ain't no social. We got work to do so get over here quick."

Terry turned away and trotted across the street to his machine and climbed on the low platform between the massive rear wheels on the steam engine.

"Let's get this train moving," Otto bellowed as he slapped the reins to his team. As soon as the supply wagon started forward, Otto pulled it out ahead of the waiting line of steam engines and threshing machines. As he passed, a sharp shriek from the whistle of the lead steamer announced the departure of the steam parade from Primrose.

The crowd quickly lost interest in the smoky assemblage as it clanked, hissed and chugged its way out of town. Gordon rode alongside and watched as Terry fed coal into the firebox of the last engine in line, but Gordon too eventually lost interest and turned his bike homeward.

The crew returned in time for supper and Terry had no trouble finding the Dewey house. Daddy always insists on proper table manners and decorum during meals. Fortunately, Terry easily fit into this practice and proved himself to be a good conversationalist as well. Mable Mae, Dorothy and little Lillian weren't unfriendly toward their new guest but kept politely aloof and reserved. Mother, on the other hand, was friendly and enjoying Terry's presence. Gordon, sitting next to Terry, asked as many questions as he thought he could get away with. There were too many and Daddy eventually asked him to stop being an "ill-mannered pest."

Eager to unpack his belongings, Terry excused himself and disappeared upstairs as soon as supper was over. Daddy went next door to his office to prepare for his next day's house calls. Little Lillian accompanied him as she often did. Mother went outside and sat at a small table on the back porch, writing a letter to her mother in Kansas. Mable Mae and Dorothy stayed behind in the kitchen doing the dishes.

Gordon ran over to the pasture to bring Stumpy Tail, the cow, home to be milked. As soon as his chore was done, he headed for the back porch where he sat down on the floor and swung his legs over the edge, dangling his feet with idle impatience, hoping Terry would come out and join him. Unanswered questions for Terry whirled in Gordon's head. Time dragged, but at last Terry emerged onto the porch, walked over to Gordon and sat down.

Small, but not short, Terry's body is muscular and well-shaped. Even sitting still, he looks nimble and strong, with muscular arms, broad shoulders, narrow waist and smooth, sun-tanned skin. Gordon, staring intently at Terry, is suddenly too shy to speak. Terry flashed a quick smile at Gordon, jumped up and dove over the edge of the porch and somersaulted back onto his feet.

"Watch this." Terry leaned over backwards until his hands touched the ground then slowly raised one leg and then the other until both feet were over his head, doing a handstand. He then flipped forward, landing upright where he whirled around, held his arms out in triumph and faced Gordon.

"Wow, were you in a circus?"

"Naw, I just like to do stuff like that. I want to join a circus someday though. Maybe after the harvest is over, I'll find one and join up. I'll fly on the trapeze."

Gordon was eager to ask more questions of Terry but held back, still smarting from Daddy's rebuke. He'd wait until tomorrow.

The sun was barely over the trees when the threshing crew gathered in front of the livery stable waiting for the trucks to pick them up. Gordon, awoke early, pulled his pillow onto the windowsill and studied the crowd, imagining the exciting dance of the threshing scene. Suddenly he jumped out of bed and began to pull on his clothes. Why hadn't he thought of it earlier, Uncle Harry's farm! He'd asked Daddy to let him go out and help when the crew threshed at Uncle Harry's!

Breakfast couldn't come soon enough for Gordon. He helped Mother get everything ready, he snatched plates away from Dorothy and set the table, he grabbed the bowls of oatmeal before Mibs could; he was like a Whirling Dervish getting breakfast underway. Daddy barely sat down when Gordon blurted out his request.

"I'm not sure they'll want you underfoot." Daddy looked at Gordon and then at Mother.

"What would you do? Help the women?" Daddy looked back at Gordon as he pondered that idea for a moment and then rejected it. "I'm inclined to grant your request but am very concerned for your safety in such a dangerous situation. What do you suggest Mother?"

"I would rather have him tied to a stake at the farm than moping around here all day."

Mother's clever reply gave Daddy just enough room to give in to Gordon's request. Tomorrow afternoon, Daddy will drive Gordon out to the farm.

Breakfast quickly evolved into a lecture on safety around whirling flywheels, long leather belts, fast moving wagons and men wielding pitch forks. The girls rolled their eyes in boredom and Gordon's mind was already on the farm so Daddy's admonitions were mostly a waste of time.

That evening, after supper, Gordon climbed the stairs slowly and quietly trying to escape detection. Reaching the top, he paused and peered down the hall toward the extra bedroom. The bedroom door was open but from where he stood, Gordon couldn't see Terry. He leaned forward and then slowly slid one foot toward the doorway. He waited, holding his breath, trying to remain undetected.

"Hey kid."

Gordon jerked in surprise.

"Quit sneaking down the hall and get in here. I want to show you something."

Gordon appeared at the doorway, grinning sheepishly. Terry was sitting cross-legged on the bed. A large, well-worn leather valise sat open in front of him. Arranged in a row across the foot of the bed was a pair of grey shirts, two pairs of pants, three undershirts and a tangle of grey socks.

"Are you a good kid?" Terry was fishing around in the valise and didn't look up. "Can you keep a secret?" Now Terry fixed his gaze on Gordon. "Well, what about it?"

"Yes." Gordon nodded. "I won't ever tell."

"Good. Have you ever seen anything like these?" Terry held out a pack of playing cards, offering them to Gordon.

Gordon took the cards, somewhat puzzled. What was so secretive about a deck of cards, the Deweys played cards all the time.

"Turn them over."

Gordon turned the cards over and gazed at the figure of a naked woman, wearing only a feathered headband, leaning casually against a marble column with one hand behind her head. Gordon looked at the next card; another naked woman, lying on a couch with her arms behind her head. Gordon kept turning the cards, each one showing a naked woman in seductive and revealing poses. Gordon had never seen a grown woman naked. He'd wondered or rather imagined what it would be like. The mysterious excitement was puzzling but pleasant.

"Don't tell your ma or your sisters. If they find out we'll be in real trouble." Terry reached out for the cards. Gordon reluctantly handed them over and Terry quickly returned the cards to the valise.

"I'll let you look at'm again sometime. Here's something else you'll like." Terry pulled a large object wrapped in black cloth out of the valise and quickly undid the cloth wrapping. Gordon gasped as Terry held up a large revolver.

"Here, Take it. It ain't loaded."

Terry held out the pistol with the butt toward Gordon. Grasping it, Gordon almost dropped it, surprised by the weight. Using both hands he finally managed to raise the barrel high enough to point the gun at the mirror over the dresser.

"Kid, you've got to eat your oatmeal if you ever want to be big enough to shoot something with that pistol. You're about as tough looking as a mosquito."

Terry's face wrinkled into a broad grin as he stared at Gordon's features, thin face, dark eyes and long lean body.

"That's what you are. You're a mosquito! That's it. I'll call you Skeeter!"

Terry laughed. Retrieving the pistol from the now-named Skeeter, he re-wrapped it in the black cloth and placed it back into the valise, snapped shut the latches, and slid the bag under the bed.

Daddy exacted his price for the generous favor, Gordon spent the next morning cleaning out the hen house and then weeding the garden. At least the tasks helped him pass the time quickly. Working in the garden also gave Gordon a chance to keep an eye on the back porch where Mother cooked on hot days. When her movements signaled the approaching dinnertime, Gordon dropped the hoe and headed for the house to clean up.

To Gordon, the trip to the farm seemed to take forever. A pall of grey straw smoke enveloped the farmyard and the cacophony of the steam engine blending with the roar of the threshing machine made it impossible to talk. As quickly as a bundle wagon heaped with shocks of wheat approached the thresher, an empty wagon was dispatched to the field to be filled.

Harry Russell, Daddy's brother-in-law, ran the farm. He took hold of Gordon and led him to where they were stacking burlap sacks of wheat. "Gordon, you can help these guys. Those bags are pretty heavy, but with one on each end you can manage.

Gordon hoped that Terry would be part of the crew, but Willy was the monkey on the crew at Harry's farm. Willy is small and wiry with mousy brown hair and a weak chin. His looks and slight build make him the butt of frequent jokes and pranks. This treatment makes Willy prickly and quick tempered.

Terry's absence left Gordon disappointed, but wheat sacks filled quickly and Gordon struggled to help get them stacked. Still, it was exciting to be at the center of the choreographed chaos of the Threshing bee.

It was late afternoon when the last bundle wagon was emptied and the massive leather belt that drove the thresher was unhooked and coiled up. Otto arrived in a truck that would haul the men back to Primrose.

The weary crew dropped into the shade of the now silent machine. Their rest was short, a sharp toot from the steam whistle signaled that the engineer was ready to back the engine toward the thresher. The threshing crew barely had time to jump up and dust themselves off before the engine chuffed and began to roll backward.

Willy jumped down from his perch behind the engine and using hand signals guided the big machine close enough to so he could grab the tongue at the front of the threshing machine and drop a stout steel pin through the tongue into a hole in the draw bar behind the engine. That done, the tractor was ready to haul the threshing machine to the next farm.

The rest of the crew climbed onto the waiting truck for the short trip to the next farm, leaving the engineer and Willy to haul the thresher.

Otto strode to the waiting steam engine, waved to the engineer. "We'll go pick up another crew and meet you two at the next farm." Otto turned back toward the truck and ran right into Willy carrying two large bundles of straw intended for the fuel box on the steam tractor. Willy staggered but kept his footing. Otto fell over Willy and onto his hands and knees.

"You clumsy little dunce, watch where you're going." Otto stood up, grabbed Willy by the arm and jerked him off his feet. As he fell, Otto kicked him.

"What'd you do that for?"

"Because you're a little runt and I felt like it. So, suck your mother's tit!"

Willy got up, brushed the dirt off and glared at Otto but made no to move to defend himself; knowing that any reply would only mean more abuse. Otto laughed and climbed up on the truck.

Threshing crews worked almost non-stop, starting as soon as the dew dried in the morning, stopping only for dinner at noon and toiling until nearly dark. Tomorrow they will be finished, twenty-four farms in six days. Two of the crews brought their tractors and engines into town that evening and would start loading them on the flatcars at sunup. Shortly after noon the two remaining crews with their machines would be at the rail yard to finish loading, working hard to get to their next stop, Petersburg, by early afternoon.

After supper, the crew members wandered one by one to the rail yard, gathering by the loading platform. Otto ordered everyone to scrounge for firewood and soon enough branches and pieces of scrap lumber were piled ready for a celebratory bonfire.
Perfumed by wood smoke, the slow twilight of evening settled over Primrose punctuated by frequent shouts and bursts of laughter from the rail yard. The celebratory sounds made it obvious that the gathering

was becoming well lubricated by more than the successful completion of the harvest.

Willy sat on a railroad tie cradling a bottle of whiskey. Suddenly, reaching over, Otto grabbed Willy's bottle. Willy made a futile attempt to retrieve it only to be rudely shoved away. Otto took a long pull and held the bottle above his head.

"Come and get it Weasel, you little piss-ant. I'd like nothing better than to squash you like a toad."

Willy was defeated. He shrank back to the far side of the fire and glowered at Otto. Otto grinning malevolently, waved the bottle with a flourish and took another swallow. Willy's anger boiled over into uncontrollable rage.

"Why don't you go back to Germany and kiss the Kaiser's ass you dirty Heine." Willy shouted over the fire. "I ain't afraid of you." Foolishly emboldened by whisky, Willy picked up a stick from the wood pile and threw it at Otto, hitting him in the chest. Otto dropped the bottle, put his hands on his hips and leaned forward toward the fire, his face reddening with rage.

"You better say your prayers Weasel, cause when I'm done, you'll be shake'n hands with the Devil."

Like a great Grizzly bear, Otto sprang directly through the fire, knocked Willy off his feet and delivered a tremendous kick to his stomach. Willy tried to crawl away but Otto grabbed him, lifted him up and slammed him to the ground.

"Stop!"

Otto turned and looked back across the fire. All eyes turned to the sound of the voice.

"I figured you was a coward the first time I saw you." Terry moved out of the shadows and closer to the fire. "If it's a fight you want, step over here."

"Mind your own business, Monkey. I'll deal with you later." Otto turned back to Willy's prostrate form.

"I said stop and I mean it." Terry shouted.

Otto turned back toward Terry, reached down, picked up the whisky bottle by the neck and broke the bottom away on a rock. Holding the jagged bottle like a dagger, Otto faced Terry.

"You miserable Monkey, I'm going to cut your gizzard out and stick it down your throat." Otto thrust the jagged bottle toward Terry.

The boom of the gunshot was so startling that everyone froze, transfixed by the explosion of sound and by the accompanying shower of sparks from the fire. With an animal-like bellow, Otto threw the bottle across the fire and took a single step after it. He stopped and clutched at his chest, his face twisted and glowering in the firelight, a black stain quickly spreading below his hands and covering his stomach. For a second, it seemed as though he would fall forward directly into the fire, but he sank onto one knee and then slowly lay over on his side emitting only a single, low moan.

The spell broken; everyone's gaze returned toward where Terry stood. As quickly as he'd appeared to challenge Otto, he'd now vanished into the shadows beyond the firelight.

The crew set about ministering to Otto, one running to alert Daddy and the others lifting Otto by his arms and legs to carry him the two blocks up Commerce Street to the Doctor's house.

Gordon awoke with a start at the sound of banging at the door. Gordon's bed was right next to the open window so he pulled his pillow over to the windowsill and leaned out far enough to see to the board sidewalk below. As Daddy opened the door, the light from his lantern slashed across the sidewalk and illuminated a breathless thresher.

"Doctor, come quick. There's a man shot bad."

"Okay. Let me get my shoes on and get my bag." The light and Daddy disappeared.

Gordon could hear footfalls, huffing and puffing of a group of men struggling up the street. As the door opened again, Daddy returned with a lantern; Gordon could now see the men carrying a large man by his arms and legs. Arriving at the door, they laid the man on the board sidewalk. Daddy set the lantern next to the man's head and put his hand on the man's neck, feeling for a pulse. Then, he reached in his bag and drew out his stethoscope which he placed on the man's chest, listening for any sign of life.

"I'm afraid he's already expired." Daddy folded the stethoscope and returned it to his bag. "Can you men carry him into my office."

The crowd wrestled Otto's body off the boardwalk and with Daddy and the lantern in the lead, disappeared into Daddy's office. They quickly re-emerged and stood expectantly.

"What happened?" Daddy held the lantern up higher so he could survey the crowd.

"Otto, the boss, got in a fight with Willy here, and Terry shot him."

"Him who? Otto or Willy?" Daddy is always careful to get his facts straight.

"Terry shot Otto."

"Where's Terry?" Daddy asked as if he expected Terry to raise his hand.

"He took off. We don't know where he is."

Daddy stopped asking questions. If Daddy realized that Terry was staying with his family, he didn't show it.

"Any of you men know where Jim McGlinchy lives?" Daddy needed to call the sheriff in Albion.

"I'm staying at the McGlinchy house."

"Wonderful. Will you be kind enough to hurry over there and tell Mr. McGlinchy that there's been a shooting and we need to telephone the sheriff right away. Inform Mr. McGlinchy that I will meet him at the depot with particulars." Daddy lowered the lantern. "The gunman having eluded capture, it seems wise that everyone retire from the streets quickly to avoid another incident." With that terse announcement, Daddy went inside with the lantern plunging the street into darkness.

Gordon was trembling with excitement. Terry shot someone! Probably with the big revolver Gordon held in his hand just three days ago. A dead body in Daddy's office! Gordon leaned back out the window as Daddy stepped out the front door carrying the lantern. Without pausing, Daddy headed down the street toward the depot. The pool of lantern light shrank quickly in the darkness.

Pulling on his pants, Gordon stepped silently into the darkness of the hallway and crept quietly down the stairs, feeling his way along the wall to the front door. He carefully opened the door, stepped outside and slowly pulled that door shut.

The street is quiet and dark, starlight providing just enough illumination to reveal black outlines and grey shapes. In the gloom, Gordon can just barely see the black spot on the board sidewalk. Bending down, he extends a finger and gingerly touches the spot, attracted and yet repulsed by the thought of a dead man's blood. The cold sensation causes him to jerk his hand away. He quickly wiped his finger on a board and turned toward Daddy's office. Tip-toeing slowly with one hand on the building wall, his stomach tightens as he reaches the door. Hoping Daddy didn't lock it, Gordon twists the knob and pushes. The door swings inward, unlocked.

The interior of the office, dark and cavernous, is silent and foreboding, devoid of shapes. Heart pounding, Gordon peers inward, straining to see into the gloom. Slowly he moves forward, sliding his feet across the floor, feeling for the desk he knows is waiting ahead. His leg brushes the desk and he slides around it, holding his hands out, searching for the wall beyond. Finding the wall, he moves along it toward the door to the examining room. At the doorway, Gordon pauses and takes a breath, shivering in terror and excitement.

The examining room is a completely black void, not the slightest shadow or shape. Gordon must move forward across the velvet darkness of the abyss with nothing to guide his movement. For a moment the boy froze. The realization that the man might be alive and Gordon's movement might awaken a monster, panic seized him and he tightened his grip on the doorway. No, he won't let himself flee; he will swallow his fear and satisfy his desire to touch the dead body. He lets go of the doorway and steps quickly forward into the darkness until he bumps the examining table.

Touching lightly, the boy explores the body, ears, hair, nose, eyes, arms and hands. Expecting a cold, clammy corpse, Gordon is surprised to find it warm and dry. As he moves along the examining table he wonders at the odor of wood smoke. Bolder now, he lingers and imagines death in a gunfight. A slight sound quickly extinguishes his bravery and causes him to jump back from the table, and he quickly retreats through the empty office and back into the street, where he sees Daddy's lantern light heading toward him from the railroad yard.

Gordon awoke with a start at the sound of a car coming up the street. It is early dawn and the sun is still below the trees and nothing is moving except the lonely vehicle trailing a dust cloud as it crunches closer. Reaching the Dewey house, the car stops right in the middle of the street and two men step out. Gordon recognizes Sheriff Anderson and guesses the other man must be a deputy. The men strode quickly to the door and knocked softly. Gordon could hear Daddy walking down the hall and opening the door.

"Morning Doctor, Sorry to get you up so early."

"Good morning to you Sheriff. The corpse is in my office, laid out on the examining table. I'll let you decide what to do with it."

"From what you said last night, the man who did the shooting is one of the threshing gang and staying here in Primrose?"

"Yes, as fate would have it, he was staying here at our house."

"Ain't that something? Can we have a look at his stuff?"

Gordon pulled back from the window, jumped off his bed, pulled open the door into the hallway and stared at the spare room door. It was closed but as he looked, it swung slowly open. Terry stood framed in the doorway. Spying Gordon, he put a finger to his lips and beckoned with his other hand. Gordon tiptoed across the hall.

"Skeeter," Terry whispered softly, "run downstairs and tell'm I'm coming right out. I don't want no trouble or nothing." He gave Gordon a gentle but urgent shove.

Gordon turned, bounded down the stairs, at the bottom step he grabbed the newel post, swung around it and landed with a bang and stopped facing the front door. The crash of Gordon's arrival as he flew around into the hall startled both Daddy and the Sheriff.

"He's upstairs and says he's coming down right now and doesn't want to make any trouble." Gordon drew a long breath, exhaled and looked upward.

Everyone stood silent, frozen by Gordon's breathless entrance and the realization that the gunman was right above their heads. The sound of Terry footfalls on the stairs broke the spell.

"Stop right there." Sheriff Anderson's voice boomed out into the hallway.

The footfalls stopped; only Terry's shoes were visible to Gordon through the balusters.

"Okay now, what are your intentions?"

"I don't want any trouble." Terry's voice was soft and low. "I'm just coming down the stairs."

"Okay now, when you get to the bottom, turn round so I can see your back and hold up your hands." The Sheriff's voice was stern and calm, inside he was shaking as he realized his gun was in its holster on the front seat of the car!

From where he stood with his back against the wall, Gordon watched as Terry stepped slowly downward. When he reached the floor, seeing Gordon, Terry smiled, winked at Gordon, put his valise down on the last step, turned around so his back was toward the door and slid sideways from the stairway into the hall.

"Damn," muttered the Sheriff under his breath. Not only was his gun in the car, so were his handcuffs. "Okay now, keep your hands over your head and back toward me."

Terry backed awkwardly down the hall, stopping as he felt the Sheriff's hand on his back.

"I'm sorry about what happened and I don't want no more trouble."

"Okay now, turn around slowly; we're going to walk outside." The Sheriff grabbed Terry's belt at the back of his trousers and pulled him around to face the street then pushed him slowly thought the door onto the sidewalk. "Hey Frank!"

At the sound of his name, Deputy Frank Willot jerked upright from his leaning position against the front fender of the car.

"Grab the handcuffs on the front seat and bring them over here." The Sheriff held tightly to Terry's belt. "Okay now young man, hold your hands out so the deputy can put those handcuffs on."

Terry held out his hands as Frank walked up and snapped on the handcuffs. The Sheriff let go of Terry's belt, relaxing a bit now that his prisoner was secured. The three men stood in the street not sure of what to do next.

Gordon picked up Terry's valise and carried it to the door. He started to step outside when he realized that all he had on was his night shirt.

"Mister Sheriff," Gordon called out, "here's Terry's clothes and things." Gordon lifted up the valise so the Sheriff could see it.

"Thanks son. I'll get it in a minute."

Gordon set the valise down in the doorway, turned and ran upstairs pulling off his nightshirt as he went. Dashing into his room, he threw the nightshirt on the floor, grabbed his pants off the chair, jerked them on, scrambled into his shirt and stuffed his bare feet into his shoes. He didn't bother tying the laces as he knew that Daddy would send him back for socks as soon as he saw the bare legs and ankles. Breathing hard, Gordon stepped to his window to see what was going to happen.

"Okay now, Frank, let's get going before the whole town shows up to watch." The sheriff turned to Terry. "What's your name son?"

"Terrance McCarron."

"Where you from?"

"Tulsa."

"Okay now, Terry, I guess that's what they call you, we're arresting you for shooting a man named Otto Grien and we're taking you to jail in Albion."

Terry, looking down, nodded and then looked up, turning his head as if wondering if anyone was watching, he saw Gordon standing in the upstairs window.

"Sheriff, can I ask you for a favor before we go?"

"Like what?"

"I promised that boy up there that I'd show him a circus trick. Is it ok if I do?"

"Okay now, we're not taking the hand cuffs off and don't do noth'n crazy either."

"Hey Skeeter," Terry called up to the window. "Watch this!"

Terry backed slowly up the street from the car, put his hands above his head and dove forward into a front somersault. As he rolled out of the somersault he sprang back to his feet, threw his hands over his head and did a one-handed cartwheel and then another. Terry looked up at Skeeter and raised his hands over his head in a salute.

"Skeeter how'd you like that?"

Gordon waved silently from the window.

"Look on your bed. I left you something."

Frank retrieved the valise, walked to the car, opened the back door and motioned to Terry to get in. As he stepped on the running board, Terry turned and looked back up at Gordon. Gordon held up his hand in a parting salute.

"So long Skeeter. Don't forget to eat your oatmeal!"

Terry climbed into the car, followed by the Sheriff. Deputy Willot stepped in front of the car, gave the crank a quick twist and retreated to the back seat. Sheriff Anderson turned the car around and slowly drove away.

Gordon looked at his bed to see what Terry left. It wasn't until he lifted his pillow that he found the deck of playing cards. He opened the box and pulled out the top card. It was the Ace of Spades with a picture of a tall, slender, Negress, clad in a flowing robe, pulled open in the front revealing all her torso. Gordon studied the picture for a few moments, slid the card back into the box and began looking over his room for a secure hiding place.

Hollyhocks

Mibs leaned back in the sofa and surveyed the comfortable living room. Lace curtains and half drawn shades dimmed and cooled the fierce afternoon sunlight. The few rays that did slip through the curtains sparkled in the crystal pendants hanging from the colored glass shade on the lamp in front of the window and made little fountains of colored light on the walls. Two overstuffed chairs accompanied by small round occasional tables, a glass fronted bookcase, a spinet, a leather covered game table, a large glass topped coffee table inlaid with mother of pearl, an oriental rug, a potted fern on a stand and Victrola nearly filled the room.

"Chaucy! Chaucy!"

A small girl in a stiff black servant's dress and white apron appeared at the doorway. "Yes Ma'am," she answered as she walked into the room.

"Dorothy is coming over for lemonade and I'd like some flowers brought in. It's so hot and I think flowers will make the room seem cooler."

"Yes Ma'am. I'll go see what's in the garden and fix you a nice bouquet." The girl disappeared as soundlessly as she'd come.

"Maybe I should change into my white dress," Mibs mused as she smoothed the fabric of her dress against the sofa. "Yes, the white dress with a blue sash and blue slippers. That will be cooler. White makes me feel cooler." She got up and walked over to the piano and slowly slid her fingers over the ivory keys. "It's too hot to play the piano. We can listen to the Victrola instead."

"Am I early?" Dorothy stood with her back against the doorway and her hands behind her head; posing like a silent film starlet. "Chaucy let me in."

"Oh Dorothy, how nice you look. Come in and sit down. Chaucy is getting some flowers and we'll have lemonade as soon as she gets back. What a lovely dress."

Dorothy's dress was sleeveless and hung loosely on her slender body, making her look even thinner. The fabric was light green silk with large white and pink flowers.

"I'm glad you like it. I saw it the last time we were in Omaha and just had to have it. Don't you think it's daring? I do!"

"It is daring! I'm so glad you could come. It seems like ages since we last talked."

Chaucy returned carrying a large oriental vase full of Hollyhocks. "There wasn't another thing blooming. The Zinnias are all shriveled up, you can't pick Morning Glories and the Snapdragons have gone to seed. These are all there is."

"Well thank you Chaucy. Put them over by the piano, next to the window. The light will bring out the color in the flowers".

The kitchen was as hot as if the stove was glowing cherry red. The curtains hung limply in the open windows begging for a little breeze. At a sturdy table in the center of the room a woman sat squeezing lemons into a large round pitcher. With a steady economy of motion, she'd pick a lemon out of a large wooden bowl, rest it on the juicer, cut it in half and squeeze the halves dry. A pile of empty lemon skins grew quickly alongside the bowl.

At last, she stopped, wiping her hands on her apron and then pulling it up, wiping her forehead. Her red hair was pulled back in a tight bun showing off her smooth white skin and friendly eyes. As she swept the yellow pile into the wooden bowl she smiled and hummed softly. As an afterthought she retrieved a few lemon halves and dropped them into the pitcher.

Carrying the pitcher over to the sink, she ladled several dippers of water from a white enamel pail and poured each slowly into the lemon juice. Then she opened the sugar jar in the pantry and added a large scoop to the pitcher. At last, it was ready.

From the cupboard she took three large glasses and set them on the sink. Opening the top of the ice box she carefully chipped a few slivers off the glistening wet block of ice, carried them to the sink and ladled just enough water over them to rinse away any unseen germs. Into the glasses went the ice and over the ice went fresh lemonade.

The woman walked out onto the back porch and stood silently in the shade and smiled as she watched the three little girls. Under the sparse shade of a large Box Elder tree, they had assembled a collection of wooden orange crates, cast off bits and pieces, a rug, a lamp and boards to mark off where the rooms of their pretend house were. Two girls sat on a crate and another stood holding an arm full of hollyhocks.

"Girls," their mother called. "Your lemonade is ready."

Sun

Father stepped onto the porch letting the screen door close behind him with a bang that echoed across the barren dirt of the empty farmyard. He raised his left hand slowly to his head, running his fingers through his hair and then reached down, picked up a straw hat lying on a chair next to the door. Stepping off the porch, he pushed the hat on and pulled the brim low to ward off the sun, leaving his pale blue eyes glinting through a mask of shadow. He stood still in the dust of the yard for a moment and looked up past the barn where his gaze stopped at the motionless windmill. Adjusting the hat still lower, he started walking toward the windmill, slowing only to pick up an empty pail next to the barn. Each footstep raised a low cloud of dust as he walked. The low Nebraska hills roll gently like an endless sea before him, hiding the prairie horizon behind waves of golden grass. What trees there are hug the bottoms along the creeks, cutting an occasional thin dark green slash between the tan hills. The bright morning sun has already pushed the sparse shade into those tree-lined crevasses leaving the hills naked, blanching against an empty blue sky. The small homestead exists in the lonely isolation of the vast prairie.

Mother sat next to the bed with a bowl of water in her lap. Morning light filtering through the drawn curtains made the room twilight and deep in shadow. On the bed, covered by a thin sheet, a small boy rested, his hair hanging in dark damp ringlets. His eyes were open, but he lay still as though deep asleep. Mother took a small cloth out of the bowl, squeezed it, folded it, and then laid the cool compress against the boy's forehead. After a bit, she pulled the cloth away and gently stroked the boy's eyes closed.

Father disconnected the windmill shaft from the pump, wiped his hands on his overalls, grasped the long-curved handle and started to pump. The slow steady squeak and groan of the pump whined through the metal frame of the windmill and drifted vacantly away. Grudgingly, a small rivulet of water splashed into the nearly empty stock tank. Breathing slowly and deeply to the rising and falling of the pump handle, Father bent to the task of filling the tank.

From the muddy shade in the remains of a small creek, cattle stirred at the pump's siren call and in thirsty anticipation they began to slowly amble toward the keening sound from the distant windmill.

The boy's breaths were short, shallow, gasps; his eyes slowly drifted back open as though he hadn't the strength to keep them closed. Mother took his hand, laid it in hers and gently stroked it. His skin was dry and hard, as though made of rough paper, his hand limp and hot to the touch. She pulled the sheet down and spread the cool cloth across his pale chest.

"It's the best I can do," she said softly as she smoothed his hair with the back of her fingers.

Father pumped steadily, wiping his face with a blue handkerchief and lifting his hat above his head to wipe his sweating forehead on a sleeve. With almost imperceptible slowness the water level in the tank rose. His shirt was soaked through with sweat when he dropped the pump handle, and the last few drops of water trickled out of the spout. The cattle quickened their pace up the hill toward the beckoning oasis as he reconnected the windmill shaft to the pump. Father filled two pails of water from the tank to refill the watering cans in the chicken yard.

The morning cool quickly fled before the triumph of the mounting sun, birds' singing slowed and then stopped altogether, leaving only the grasshoppers' sizzling buzz to accentuate the heating air; the distant hilltops now dancing in heat-wave frenzy.

Leaving the chicken yard, Father picked up a white enamel kitchen pail from the shade of the barn, filled it from the yard pump and then walked back to the barn, stopping next to a ladder that led to the roof. He looked up, adjusted his hat and began to climb, carrying the pail with one hand and holding on to the ladder with the other. On the roof several bundles of shingles were spread out uniformly. Behind one stood a keg of nails, Father cautiously walked to it and set the pail down next to the nail keg. He picked up a dipper and dropped it in the pail, lifted a carpenter's apron out of the nail keg, tied it on and slipped a hammer into the loop on the leg of his overalls.

Creeping gingerly across the steep roof he worked his way back to where he left off the day before.

The shingles were already almost too hot to touch, yet he worked without gloves. Sliding a shingle off the pile, he'd quickly position it and nail it down with three nails - thump, bang - thump, bang - thump, bang. When he'd gone as high up the roof as he could reach, he moved over and started another column. He worked steadily, stopping only to move bundles of shingles or for a dipper of water from the pail or to get more nails from the keg.

Mother took a spoon, filled it with water from the bowl and held it to the boy's lips, letting the water slowly dribble into his mouth. He caught his breath and then swallowed. She nodded encouragingly and gave him another spoonful which he also swallowed. On the third spoonful he gagged, and she quit.

"When the fever passes, you'll get better. I'll keep you cool until the fever passes. I'll keep you cool." She lifted the cloth out of the bowl, squeezed it, folded it and laid it gently across his forehead and then stroked his eyes closed.

The noonday sun burned away the last meager patches of shade; cattle retreated into the willow thickets in the drying mud of the creek bottom, chickens fluffed in the dust on the north side shade of the henhouse. Father untied his carpenter's apron, retrieved the water pail, climbed slowly down the ladder and walked across the dusty yard. He set the pail down on the chair by the door and washed his hands in the remaining water. Finishing, he picked up the pail and emptied it in the small garden next to the porch. Dropping his hat on the chair he went inside.

She had prepared his dinner; cold boiled potatoes, a slice of ham, peach sauce and nectar. He ate mechanically, paying little attention to the food. Setting the empty dishes on the pantry he walked to the bedroom. He stopped at the doorway, his hands in his back pockets, and looked down at the mother and the boy.

"He's not getting any better." Mother pushed her hair from her forehead with the back of her hand. "What can we do?" Her pleading eyes sought him.

Father stared silently and then turned away; her question had no answer.

With a fresh pail of water and two feed sacks he climbed back onto the barn roof. The whole countryside shimmered in the still heat. Using the feed sacks for protection from the hot shingles, he knelt down and the steady hammering resumed.

The blue sky slowly disappeared behind the flaming white corona of the sun. Everything was hot to the touch, even the handle of the dipper in the water pail. The heat of the roof burned through the soles of his shoes if he stood too long.

The hammering stopped. He crawled over to the water pail, took off his hat and poured a dipper full of water over his head and face. Pulling his hat back on his head he stood and scanned the horizon like a Bedouin in the desert. In the distance a bird speck caught his gaze - hawk or turkey vulture or eagle - he watched as it slowly circled, riding a thermal in an upward spiral, growing smaller and smaller until its final dot is lost in the white-hot vault of the sky.

Sunlight on the window shade colored the bedroom ocher, turning it into a vision of the fiery furnace. In the reddish gloom the boy on the bed seemed to glow with a feverish incandescent red heat. Mother fanned the boy, his breathing now a low dry whisper. She dribbled a little water into his mouth, he barely swallowed. She ran her fingers through his damp hair and behind his hot, dry ears, leaning over, she talked quietly of flowers and shade and cool nectar and cookies and dew on the grass and laughter and butterflies. Slowly his eyes closed, slowly his whispered breathing diminished, slowly he cooled and relaxed.

"He's gone." At the sound of her whispered call across the yard the hammering stopped.

Father drank a dipper of water, flinging the last few drops over the roof. Dropping the dipper back into the pail he climbed down the ladder, went into the barn and came out with a shovel.

"I want him by the flowers."

He walked to the spot and started to dig, thrusting the shovel into the dry dusty ground. A mound of gravely dirt grew quickly beside the Zinnias and Pansies.

She wrapped the boy in a sheet, carefully folding it around his small body and then laid the shrouded bundle on the white quilt her mother made, the one with the blue Morningstar pattern; the one the boy liked so much.

The grave finished, he walked to the porch, dropped his hat on the chair by the door and went inside, going straight to the bedroom. Seeing the quilted bundle on the bed, he turned and walked back to the kitchen, pulled open a pantry drawer and took out a feed sack and returned to the bedroom.

"We need the quilt, he don't." He handed the feed sack to the woman.

Without a word she undid the quilt and unwrapped the sheet. Together they pulled the sack around the boy. When they finished, she sewed the sack shut.

Cradling the sack in his arms the man carried the boy out through the kitchen, across the porch and laid him on the ground between the flowers and the grave. Together, Father at the head and Mother at the feet, they lowered the small bundle gently into the ground. Father got up and reached for the shovel, but Mother, still kneeling, grasped his arm and he paused.

"The Book says He'll take you to still waters," she looked down at the boy. "The Book says not to be afraid; He'll comfort you. He says," she paused. "He says," she choked silently, let go of the man's arm and put her hands to her face so only her downcast eyes showed.

Grimly she knelt, watching each shovel full of dusty dirt slowly obliterate the gay colors of the feed sack. When the last corner of the sack disappeared, she covered her eyes.

After the grave was mounded full, he took the shovel back to the barn and then climbed the ladder up to the roof. As he reached the top he looked back toward the flowers. Mother still knelt at the foot of the grave mound.

The sun was far to the west when he stopped shingling. The woman had gone inside leaving a small bouquet of flowers on the grave. He took off the carpenter's apron and put it and the hammer on the nail keg. Picking up the water pail, he climbed slowly down the ladder and walked back across the yard to the house and onto the porch. He reached for his hat, ready to drop it on the chair by the door. Then he saw the shoes under the chair.

They were small and dusty and run-over, the laces were frayed and caked with dried mud; boys' shoes, climbing shoes, exploring shoes, chasing shoes, waiting shoes, empty shoes.

He put his hat back on and picked up the shoes. He turned them over and looked at the soles, as though wondering what to do with them. He shrugged slightly, nodded his head, and then walked back to the barn.

Returning with the shovel, he walked over to the grave, put the shoes on top next to the bouquet of flowers and started to dig at the foot of the mound. When he had almost reached the feed sack he put the shovel down, picked up the shoes, reached down into the hole and pushed the dirt away with his hands until he could feel the cloth. He put the shoes underneath the sack and tucked it down around them. He quickly refilled the hole and returned the shovel to the barn.

Slowly he retraced his steps across the dusty yard and stepped heavily onto the porch. Without thinking he pulled his hat off and reached over to drop it on the chair. He paused for a moment, looking down, then dropped the hat, pulled the screen door open and stepped inside, shutting the screen door softly.

Lengthening shadows slowly slide out from under the blue-green twilight of the western hills. To the north, creamy clouds drift over the Niobrara River and an orange moon climbs in the dark-blue eastern sky as the now ruddy sun settles into the opposite horizon. With a discordant squeak, the windmill fan begins to grudgingly rotate as a warm evening breeze rustles softly across the twilight.

Goodbye Sweet Primrose

The smell of coffee and frying bacon gradually won out over sleep and I opened my eyes to the half-light of early morning. Mom had complained that lately she'd been sleeping in fits and starts so I wasn't surprised that she was already up. She'd never admit to excitement, but I knew she was looking forward to our day.

As I came out of the bedroom Mom saw me and smiled. Last year when I admitted to myself that Dad was losing out to old age, I suggested that we should all take one more trip together; one last excursion to Dad's boyhood home in Charles City, Iowa.

"The coffee's ready and I've got some toast in. By the time you're done in the bathroom I'll have your breakfast ready."

"I'll be out in a jiffy." I cleaned up quickly and headed back to the kitchen.

We agreed to go to Charles City on Memorial Day. In January, Dad died, spoiling our plan by slipping away peacefully in his sleep. So, I made the same offer to Mom, a trip to the place she grew up, Primrose, Nebraska. It would be just the two of us and we knew we'd have to make an early start.

"It's supposed to rain and it sure looks like it. I hope you can get the lilacs cut before it starts." Mom held back a curtain and peered out at the grey sky. She returned to the stove, dished up some bacon strips and two eggs and handed me the plate.

As I ate, Mom made sandwiches and packed a lunch box with fruit, cookies and the sandwiches.

"Do you want another egg or some more bacon?"

"Mom, do I look like I need another egg?"

"I know. I miss cooking for Steve. It's no fun eating alone and breakfast was your dad's favorite meal. We always had eggs and bacon on Sunday morning after church." Mom stood looking at me, her expression suddenly melancholy and then turned back to the stove and began gathering up her cooking utensils.

"I'm going to get the lilacs." I pushed away my plate, stood up and headed for the back door.

Spring had been late and cool so the lilac bushes in the back yard were still in full bloom, unusual for Memorial Day weekend in southern Minnesota. I filled a pail with water and got the pruning shears from the garage. The air was damp and heavy, but warm under a grey and lowering sky. The fragrance of the flowers surrounded me as I plunged into the bushes. I worked fast and had the pail full in a few minutes. When I got back to the garage, I wrapped the stems in wet rags and then carefully put the flowers in a plastic bag. By the time I was finished Mom was at the door with the lunch bag.

We packed the car quickly and headed west into a darkening sky; soon heavy rain blotted out the southwestern Minnesota countryside leaving us to drive suspended in the twilight of mist. For the first few miles we talked -- speculating about the cemetery at Albion, where Mom's parents are buried, the roads in Nebraska, how long it would take to get to Primrose; but the rumble of the rain and the steady rhythm of the windshield wipers silenced us, transformed our excitement and anticipation into a dogged unspoken determination, each a captive of our private thoughts.

"I'm glad you're driving. Dad hated driving in the rain. He was a good driver though. Last year when that boy ran out in front of us, he had to drive clear up onto the boulevard to miss him. He slowed down at night. He was a good driver."

"How many times did you tell me that you worried about his driving? I thought you were afraid he'd kill someone."

"Well, he started to forget where he was going. I guess I just worry."

"Dad always forgot where he was going and you always worry too much. I'll bet you still worry about your sons changing their underwear."

"You always make me laugh. Did you put on clean underwear this morning?" Mom shook her head and chuckled.

We planned on getting to the cemetery in Albion before lunch, that would give us plenty of time in Primrose and a chance to drive around Cedar Rapids too (Dr. Dewey moved his practice and family to Cedar Rapids, Nebraska in 1923). The rain slowed us down and then a detour put us on rough, narrow roads and added twenty miles to the trip. We finally stopped at Norfolk, Nebraska, out of gas, out of coffee and longing for a bathroom. Mom bought us some coffee and a couple of donuts while I gassed up the car.

"It's after ten already. We'll never make it to Albion before noon. This is just awful." Mom got in the car, closed the door and looked at me, crestfallen.

"No big deal, Mom. You sound like the cemetary'll be gone if we don't make it there before twelve." I smiled at her and started the car.

"Oh, I know what you mean, but Mibs wants us to be at her place before six and that's such a long way to go. I don't want her to worry if we're late."

"Do they have phones in Lincoln? If we're going to be late let's call her."

It was still raining when we got to Albion. I didn't know where the cemetery was and Mom couldn't remember so we had to stop at a gas station and ask directions -- south on the next street, can't miss it.

"One time I rode up here from Cedar Rapids with some friends. My girlfriend had borrowed her father's car and nobody knew where we were. She went through a stop sign and ran into another car. I had to call Daddy for a ride home. I think it was after midnight. He was so mad he could hardly talk."

"When we came up here for the Boone County Fair we'd spend the entire day. Mom would make a lunch of fried chicken and Daddy would give us each a dollar to spend. We felt rich with a whole dollar. I liked the merry-go-round best. Oh gosh that was fun."

The rain dwindled to a mist as we drove into the cemetery. Mom got a hand drawn map out of her purse and studied it as we drove up toward the top. The Albion cemetery sticks upward out of the prairie like an ancient burial mound crowned with tall pine trees and studded with gravestones that march in irregular rows as though defying any attempt at order.

"We went in the wrong gate. I thought this didn't look right. Can we drive down there to that other gate and go up that road toward the top? Go slow. I'm not quite sure how to follow Dot's map." Mom held her drawing up looking for a landmark.

I drove slowly to the other gate and turned back uphill.

"There it is! See the big tombstone with the round thing on top. Now drive until it's lined up with that other big one over there by the trees." Mom showed me her map, drawn long ago by her sister, Dorothy. I drove forward until the stones lined up and then stopped.

Mom got out and walked slowly uphill, angling across the rows of markers. She stopped and waved me toward her.

"Here they are right where the map showed they were." Mom smiled triumphantly and pointed down.

I got out the lilacs, took a jug of water out of the trunk and walked over to Mom. There were metal vases sunk alongside each grave marker; I pulled them up and Mom arranged the flowers and then poured in some water.

"Won't people be surprised when they see lilacs? They're all done blooming down here. Don't they look nice?"

We stood back, admiring our work, oblivious to the misty rain.

"Didn't the monument company do a nice job of matching Gordon's stone to Daddy and Mother's?"

Mom's older brother, Gordon, had died a few years before. He was cremated I believe, but everyone agreed that there should be a stone in the family plot. "After all the trouble I had getting his ashes here I wasn't too sure what they'd do about a stone."

We finished with the flowers, took pictures of each other and walked back to the car. Mom got out the lunch box and handed me a sandwich. We ate in silence. The mist drifted away, and pale sunlight brightened the flowers and flags and wreaths. From our vantage we watched as the growing sunlight began to attract cars into the cemetery and soon little knots of people searched through the tombstones, gathered when they found the right one and performed their memorial rituals as we had done.

"Let's get going. I'm anxious to get to Primrose."

I guess Mom didn't want to speculate about when she'd come back to the Albion cemetery or at least she didn't want to say anything about it. I wondered what she was thinking but kept my questions to myself.

Primrose, an English name that seems ill-suited to the prairies of Nebraska. It evokes cottages surrounded by the flowers of the same name. Alas, what's left of Primrose was barely visible from the road, a long-vacant brick schoolhouse, a weed-grown playground and a boarded-up community center. We drove past these ancient ruins, around the corner onto a deserted main street, with the no longer appropriate name, Commerce Street. A tornado in the mid-sixties finished off what decay had begun before the great depression. Primrose was born at the turn of the century, flourished briefly, and wilted, a victim of the motorcar. The tornado destroyed nearly everything left in the town and there was no need to rebuild. As a kind but foolish gesture of support, the disaster relief program built the community center next to the vacant school, now it, too. is vacant.

"When I was a little girl, I used to roller-skate on this sidewalk." Said Mom. "I'd go way up to the end and skate downhill all the way past our house to the bank. One morning I got sick and went home from school. By afternoon I felt better so I put on my skates and went up to the end of the sidewalk and started skating down. Just as I got by the school my teacher came walking along. She stopped and looked at me. I could have died right there. I said `I got better' and skated right past her."

We drove up to the end of the street and stopped in front of an overgrown thicket of brush and trees. Nearly invisible in the dim recesses of the thicket was a large house, or rather the moss-covered corpse of a once grand house. Trees grew though the porch, the rotted roof sagged, and empty, dark windows stared at nothing.

"I used to come up here and play. They had electricity and indoor plumbing. Once I even stayed for dinner. I think he owned the bank."

I turned the car around and we drove back down the street.

"Daddy's office was right about here."

I pulled over to the side and stopped.

"Our house was right next door. I suppose the tornado blew them down."

At the place where Mom said her Dad's office had been, stood a small building with a single window and a glass door. The sign hanging in the door proclaimed `PRIMROSE VOLUNTEER LIBRARY.'

"Let's go in Mom. Who knows what we'll find." I didn't wait for her answer, opened the car door and got out.

A pleasant-looking lady sat at a small table, surrounded by shelves of paperback books. Mom and I took up most of the available floor space in the tiny room. Before the lady could greet us, Mom spoke.

"I grew up in Primrose. I think my father's office stood on this spot. He was a doctor, Doctor Dewey. My name is Lillian, Lillian McCauley."

"Oh, my gracious, I'm so glad to meet you. My husband grew up here, but I haven't lived here very long. I'm going to call my friend Ethelyn; she's lived here all her life. I'll bet she'll want to meet you."

"Oh, don't bother. We're staying just a few minutes."

"It's no bother." She picked up the phone and began dialing.

"She'll be right over. She thinks she knows you."

In a few minutes Ethelyn arrived and crowded into the room. I edged around the table looking for vacant floor space. Glancing down at a stack of books on a table crowded into a corner, a book caught my eye, "The History of Boone County." I idly thumbed through it while waiting for our visitor. She soon arrived, wreathed in smiles and quickly gave Mom a hug.

"Lillian Dewey! Your Dad delivered me! I remember you. Yes, you were the nurse, weren't you?"

"No, you must be thinking of someone else."

"Mom," I said. "Give her a chance to talk, I think she's right."

Mom had gone to nurse's training after high school but got sick and couldn't finish. As a young girl she had often gone on house calls to help her dad. Something told me Ethelyn was on the right track.

"You sat up all night with my brother Harry and nursed him. I know it was you. Do you remember Harry Hanson?"

"Yes, I remember him. He had heart trouble and couldn't lie down and couldn't sleep. I think I spent several nights with him before he died. That was a long time ago. Harry Hanson. He was so nice."

"Well, he was my older brother. I remember you coming over and sitting with him. I'm sure glad to see you again, it brings back the old days. There isn't much left of Primrose now is there." She paused, looked out the window, and then turned back to Mom. "A tornado went right down Main Street in 1969 and took just about everything. Everyone ran down to the cafe and got in the vault -- it used to be the bank."

"What happened to the Methodist Church?"

"It burned down before the tornado. I guess everyone just switched to being Presbyterian. The school closed in the seventies. They built the Community Center with disaster relief money from the tornado but that closed too. We've pretty much disappeared."

I think it took a while for Mom to realize that to them she was remembered as a nurse -- probably the only nurse that Primrose ever had. As she talked, Mom's expression slowly changed as that realization sank in, until she was beaming with joy. I became so fascinated watching her that I didn't pay any attention to what anyone talked about. In the end we said our goodbyes and returned to the car.

"Isn't it wonderful," said Mom as I started the car. "After all these years to meet someone who actually remembers you. Isn't it wonderful? I'm so glad we came back."

I backed the car into the street and drove southward, out of town. When we got to the highway I stopped and looked back at Primrose. Through the veil of trees, the sunlight seemed to brighten the town, making it look clean and neat and alive, as though Mom's visit had rejuvenated it for just a moment.

We drove away and Primrose was soon lost in the low hills and tree-lined creek banks. For a while we drove in silence, savoring our brief encounter with Primrose.

"Do we have time to go through Schuyler?" Mom opened her purse and took out a slip of paper, another old hand drawn map. "Cousin Harriet sent me a map of the cemetery there that shows where my great grandparents are buried, Wilcox was their name."

I nodded in agreement.

"Isn't it wonderful?"

Do we really know who we are? Are we what we see in the mirror? Are we what we think of ourselves? Or are we the sum of the memories that trail behind us like the wake of a ship -- spreading slowly across our lives, fading but never really disappearing?

After all this time Mom discovered that she was a nurse after all -- not because she'd actually graduated from nurse's training, but because everyone in Primrose remembered her as the nurse. It is wonderful.